Somewhere in Minnesota

For my family

Somewhere in Minnesota

Órfhlaith Foyle

Somewhere in Minnesota

is published in 2011 by
ARLEN HOUSE
an imprint of Arlen Publications Ltd
42 Grange Abbey Road
Baldoyle
Dublin 13
Ireland
Phone/Fax: 353 86 8207617
Email: arlenhouse@gmail.com
arlenhouse.blogspot.com
www.arlenhouse.com

Distributed internationally by
SYRACUSE UNIVERSITY PRESS
621 Skytop Road, Suite 110
Syracuse, NY 13244–5290
Phone: 315–443–5534/Fax: 315–443–5545
Email: supress@syr.edu

978–1–85132–030–1, paperback
978–1–85132–032–5, hardback

Typesetting ¦ Arlen House
Cover Images ¦ Dymphna Tate

CONTENTS

Acknowledgments

'Somewhere in Minnesota' was first published in *New Irish Short Stories* edited by Joseph O'Connor (Faber & Faber, 2011). Many thanks to Joe for his kind and generous words.

Earlier versions of these stories were first published in the following publications. Many thanks to the editors and publishers:

'Runt', in *The Stinging Fly* Issue 11 (Winter 2008/09).
'The Secret Life of Madame Defarge', in *Horizon Review* 3 (2009).
'Sweet Frankie', in *DIVAS! A Sense of Place* (Arlen House, 2005).
'Journey Back', 'New Bodies for Old', 'Two Vampires', 'The Extraordinaire', 'Sweat and Feet', and 'An Incident in the Bedroom', in *Revenge* (Arlen House, 2005).

Thanks to my publisher Alan Hayes at Arlen House for his encouragement, advice and support.

SOMEWHERE IN MINNESOTA

Somewhere in Minnesota

I was sitting in a diner in god-knows-where in Duluth, Minnesota during wintertime and the waitress was concerned for me. She liked my accent and noticed my bruised face.

She said: 'Who's been hurting you, sweetheart?'

I don't like it when people use sweet language on strangers. Sweet language belongs to lovers. But she was kind. A little bit old with worn blonde hair, the sort that was dying before she was and the fat had fallen in her face. I wanted to draw her, so I ripped a napkin from the dispenser and took my pencil from my pocket. My phone buzzed against my hip twice then switched to message mode.

The diner door opened and the waitress called out, 'Hey John'.

John raised a salute. 'How are you these days, Hetty? The kids?'

Hetty laughed. She said her husband had come over with the kids yesterday. She said they were all grown up now and one of them wanted to be an archaeologist. He always did like finding dead useless things, she said.

I tried to ignore her voice, but it had a good rhythm to it and it helped me move my pencil.

Hetty called over, 'You okay there, girl?'

I don't know if she wanted John to see me or maybe she just didn't want to talk about her kids and husband anymore but she made John look.

Now some men you just know they like to see hurt women. John stared right at me and the muscles jumped across his jaw and his eyes lit, before his head went back down over the menu.

I glanced to where Hetty was pouring coffee for some other customer. Her arms bulged from beneath her little-girl waitress uniform. Her earrings chimed and she was singing along to the radio. A few minutes later, she served John his coffee and his 'usual'.

The diner was big and bright and the voices were loud. My phone buzzed again. I had lost count by now. I finished drawing and watched an old man talk into his chicken dinner. Bits of chicken fell from his beard and his knee was jiggling hard under his table.

'How are you getting on?' Hetty called over to me. I curled my hand over my napkin and on she came, high heels clicking fast, and I saw John raise his expression from his coffee to my face.

I gave him a smile. He fit a potato from his fork to his mouth.

When I was a little girl my mother said that I watched people too much. I made them scared and angry, she said. But it was just the way my mind turned when it saw something it liked.

Hetty was humming 'You are my Sunshine' as she reached me. She stopped humming as soon as she saw what I had done.

I had made her younger with darker hair similar to what I had seen growing from her roots and I had fluffed it about her head because it made her neck longer that way. I had corralled the fat from under her chin and re-planted it in her cheeks. I had widened her eyes, so that she looked as innocent as she might have been once.

'Do you like it?' I asked.

Hetty snatched it and held it aloft. 'Hey John, we've an artist here'.

John stuck his head out from his neck and focussed on the napkin.

'Looks just like you did this morning, Hetty'.

Hetty laughed and folded the napkin into her apron pocket. Then she tried to touch my face, and my insides crept to my backbone. I stood up fast and nearly fell into her.

She took hold of me. 'Take it easy, sweetheart'. She clucked her tongue. 'Who did this to you?'

I said: 'The ladies, please?'

Hetty started to bring me towards the back of the diner, but I stopped her.

'Just show me please'.

Hetty dropped her arms from me. Her voice went sharp. 'What's your name?'

'Frankie', I told her.

She held her hands just beneath my chin, but not touching me. 'You go in there and take as long as you please, Frankie. Food is on me'.

The ladies room smelled of synthetic cherries. It had pale green walls and there were false blue and pink flowers stuck in a yellow vase on a shelf beside the sink's mirror. I locked the door and stripped to my slip. I filled the sink with cold, cold water. I just wanted to freeze the pain inside me. I dampened the corner of my blouse and patted at the blood on my forehead.

The diner music piped into the air above me. I stared at my face. My phone buzzed. Peter's name was flashing, so I answered.

'Hey', I said.

'Whereabouts are you?' he said.

'Somewhere in Minnesota', I answered.

'Christ, Frankie, just tell me you're still in Duluth'.

I stared at my reflection as I dabbed at my face with one hand while I held the phone in the other. Peter's voice babbled on. He mentioned 'crisis' more than once. He mentioned money a little bit more. He took a breath and I waited. I put my left hand into the freezing water and felt the cold on my wrist.

'Frankie, just come back'.

I heard the background noise of music and glasses and people's voices. I almost saw the tall white walls holding my paintings and the shiny clean skin of everyone there.

'Frankie, just come back now'.

I said nothing and waited. Peter breathed in and out.

'Fuck your father, Frankie', he said.

I waited some more seconds, then I switched off the phone.

The piped music stopped, then sputtered on. My face was beginning to swell. I ran my tongue over my lips to feel the sting. I knew I'd have to go outside, finish whatever Hetty had cooked for me and make some kind of conversation Minnesota Americans would appreciate. I'd ease on into their lineage, find an Irish link and marvel it big. They liked it big here.

'Hey, Frankie … you still in there?' A man's voice came through the wall.

So I answered, 'Yes?'

'You okay?' said his voice.

'I'm fine, yes'.

'I'm going to piss', he continued. 'And the acoustics in here are astronomical'.

I rested against the sink as the sound of piss rivered through the wall.

Hetty knocked on the door. 'You okay in there, honey?'

I heard her giggle and say, 'Hey, John, watch where you put your hands'.

I looked at the mirror and whispered, 'Hey, John, watch where you put your hands'.

I smoothed down my hair, then went back out. John watched me sit and Hetty came over with the food.

The chicken on the plate seemed alive. It glistened up from under slow-moving brown gravy. Boiled greens hung on its thighs and there was some potato mashed into the shape of a deflated ball, burnt on the edges, smeared in yellow cheese. I willed the chicken to stop moving. I counted to ten with my eyes closed and felt something move in front of me. When I opened them, John was seated opposite. He had his coffee and apricot pie.

He said, 'Eat the chicken. It's good'.

I peeled off some thigh meat with my knife, then covered it in mash.

'Hetty does the best gravy', John said.

He cut a chunk from his pie and stuck it in his mouth. He had a nice mouth. Thin but well curved. I decided not to talk just yet and maybe he appreciated the tension because he smiled and hummed a little, then glanced over to Hetty who winked at us both.

'She's been married five times', John mentioned. 'Only one of her husbands gave her kids. She loves those kids, but she can't stand having them for more than three days'.

I nodded and continued to shave meat and mash together.

'That's the thing about Hetty', John said. 'She can act the love just as long as she's not near it too often'.

He smiled and pointed his fork at my face. 'So you coming in here looking like that gets her mother instincts all in a tizzy'.

'You and Hetty', I stated.

He shrugged. 'We're friends'. He smiled. 'We like meeting people'.

I nodded and chewed on chicken. John smiled at my bruises and cut an apricot in two with the side of his spoon.

'Hetty likes to help people. So do I'.

I said nothing while I scraped a square of cheese from my mash.

'I'm just here to eat', I told him.

John smiled and shook his head. 'With a face like yours you should be in hospital, but you're not. Makes me and Hetty wonder'.

I glanced around the perimeter of the diner. I noted how far I was from the main entrance and a thin delight of fear ran from my throat to my guts. I breathed in and kept smiling. The old man caught my smile and raised his hand in greeting. A group of silent kids were reading comics in another booth. I had picked the diner because I had thought it seemed the sort of place people got lost in for a while.

'I've just left my boyfriend', I said.

John nodded. 'He do that?'

'No'.

'Then who did?'

The chicken and mash turned sour in my throat, as I swallowed it down.

'I did this to myself', I admitted out loud.

John's eyebrows rose. He looked across at Hetty and her smile slid from him to me.

I glanced at my phone. I told myself five more minutes, or maybe desert and coffee, then I'll ring back.

After Peter first saw my paintings, he wanted to know where my father was.

'Dead', I told him.

Peter had dark hair and green eyes. I had watched him move about the gallery like a long cat on longer legs. I presumed him gay, but what he really was was a boy who just wanted to love somebody like me.

'I kidnap men on a regular basis', I half-warned.

'I don't mind', he half-promised and smiled like a boy from a fairy tale. He stood under a painting of mine, a backbone with arrowed sinews, and said it was as if I was drawing the birth of a ghost.

John kept digging pieces from his pie, but looked at me from under his eyes. Hetty smiled over. Her earrings jangled and she gave me the thumbs up. She reached behind the counter, then held the *Duluth Tribune* open to the arts section. My normal face was there.

'You're famous', she stage-whispered at me.

I smiled at her. She was nothing like my mother. My mother told me I looked like my father as I slept. She said I had more of his genes in me than any of her other children. She said once he had finished with me, I was like something poisonous. She said what he put in me I'd keep in me forever.

Hetty came over to our table with more coffee.

'How come you're not where you're supposed to be?' she asked.

I didn't answer.

'You like the chicken?'

'It's good', I lied to her.

I glanced at her blue eye shadow and her white-flour soft face. Her lipstick was peeling. John pushed his hand towards mine, waited a second, then finger-tipped my knuckles.

I didn't like that. I didn't like the way he played on my fingers where rings should be, where things that twinkle with good love should be.

'It's my father's anniversary', I blurted.

'For what?' John asked.

'He died three years ago'. I said.

Hetty coughed. She tapped her fingers on the table, then on her mouth. 'Hey, let's get wine after I finish up here', she suggested.

John smiled. 'Tash will be worried if I'm too late'.

Hetty glanced at me. 'His fiancée', she explained.

She sat in beside me, slipped off her shoes and reached down to rub her nylon toes. A smell rose from them and I helped myself to more coffee.

'I can be late for a bit', John said. He had dry skin and his fingers were ragged. He saw me looking. 'I work with wood', he said. 'Sometimes the resin reacts with my skin'.

'Need to hand it over to someone', Hetty picked a string of chicken from my plate and laid it on her tongue. 'Fifty means you're not so young'. She elbowed me, 'but don't he look good for fifty? Like a really old thirty-year old'.

She giggled and the chicken string spat out of her mouth and onto the table. She picked it up, rolled it into a ball between her fingers, then dropped it to the floor.

'Hey', she remembered and pulled out the napkin from her apron pocket. 'You've got to sign this'. She handed me her waitress pen and I signed my name under the sketch. She tried to touch my cheek.

'So ... who did that?' she said and settled her fingers into a small claw over the napkin.

I gave her back her pen. 'It doesn't matter'.

Hetty smiled large at John.

'She looks like your Tasha, don't she, John? Just like you want to bundle her up in your arms and take her home'.

'Tasha wouldn't like that', John guessed.

'We can go to my place', Hetty decided.

'What would we do there?' I asked.

Hetty stroked her finger along my left hand. 'You're cold', she said, 'we could warm you up'.

'It *is* too late', I said. I hunched my shoulders in, then said, 'the last time I did this, I was in Florence'.

'Oh yeah', Hetty said with her big, bright smile and her teeth flashed with clean saliva.

'His name was Matthias. He was Swiss-German. He was very polite'.

John and Hetty didn't say anything.

I took out my phone and switched it on.

Hetty took it from me and ran through its call list. 'Who's Peter?'

'Turn it off', John told Hetty and held his hand out for it.

'I don't do threesomes', I said.

Hetty went back to stroking my hand. John smiled.

'Doesn't matter', Hetty said, 'we can just talk'. She touched the side of my face. 'Maybe we could give you a bath, we could clean you up'.

I kept on eating. Hetty got impatient. She sucked her tongue against her teeth and hummed. John was waiting for me to say something. I stared at his face. This close he looked old and too soft, the sort of softness that I didn't want to touch. I thought of my father and the skin beneath his eyes.

So I said, 'I paid a ten-year-old boy to beat me up today'.

My jaw clicked on a tiny chicken bone. John stared at my bruises and the faint colour of blood over my face. I stared right into his eyes.

'A ten-year-old', I insisted.

Hetty growled at me. 'What kind of game are you playing?'

She kicked John underneath the table. He coughed and sloshed his coffee. I was tired. The pain was fading except for the headache at the back of my skull and I pressed the top of my spine hard against the back of my seat.

'Hey', John barked.

I looked at him. I saw him trying to screw some kind of threat into his eyes, but I didn't want to play after all. I yawned and stretched my jaw and the pain rose like nails into the back of my skull.

'He liked my colouring pencils', I explained.

Hetty's face went slack under her make-up. 'What the ...?'

John warned her, 'I don't have time for this'.

He put my phone back down on the table. Hetty shifted to the edge of her seat, fluffed out her hair over her forehead, then took away my knife and fork.

I glanced from John's face to hers. 'And I paid him ten dollars', I told them.

John rubbed his watch against his chin. He was too old to react the way Peter had done. He didn't admire the perverse romance of it all.

Peter had stayed. Peter had promised to make me new again, but failed. Peter ... who sat at a table in Florence and said he didn't want this game anymore.

Peter looked at me. 'I don't think you want love, Frankie. I don't think you're built for it'. He poured some wine. 'Maybe you should just leave me one day. Maybe I could take it'.

John slapped his hand on the table top. He stood up. 'No psychos', he said. 'Not anymore'.

'But she's pretty', Hetty started to negotiate, yet she was half-standing and her toes were crawling for her shoes.

John gave her a look so she stood up, cracked her towel against the edge of the table and lowered her face close to mine.

'I never liked bitches like you'.

I looked up at her. I could see holes in her skin where the make-up had dripped off from the heat of her grill.

'All waiting to be patched up like dogs', she spat. She sucked up the dribble on her lips and I put my hand over my coffee cup when she grabbed my plate.

John was talking to the old man. Hetty went back behind the diner bar and began wiping it. I watched everyone's movements in slow motion.

John walked out of the diner.

Hetty turned up the radio.

The old man winked at me. I glanced at his hands inside his fly. The old man laughed and Hetty flicked out the newspaper into the air before shaping it, edge to edge, on the diner counter. The comic book kids got up and walked out.

I rang Peter. Then I remained in place, watching the dark night outside the diner's windows and the car lights looping backwards and forwards like mad eyes with nothing to hold them.

The last time my father hit me I was twenty-one-years-old. He stood back and waited a few seconds before he fixed my hair behind my ears.

The little boy had said, 'If it hurts, will you cry?'

'No', I said.

He shifted on his heels and looked towards the far end of the playground.

'Are you crazy?' he said.

'No, just sometimes I feel better when I'm hurt'. I smiled up at the sky. It was drained of sun. 'And my boyfriend gets tired sometimes'.

'Oh, okay', said the boy.

So I lay on the ground to make it easy for him. I could hear his feet slip in the mush of snow, then his fist bounced into my face. The shock lifted my chest.

'Harder', I said.

The boy's fists punched into my face. I breathed each time and when I tasted too much blood, I pushed him away.

He fell back and snarled.

I sat up and watched the world slide in and out of focus. I could hear the cars growl on the street beyond the park's wall. Someone yelled for someone and I knew if it was Peter yelling for me, then it would be too early. I needed the pain first.

'You okay?' the boy said. He danced on his feet.

I said nothing for seconds. The boy kicked about and glanced toward a group of adults at the far end of the play area. Then he shoved his fists into his coat pockets and looked at me.

'Where's my money?'

I took my purse from my coat pocket and handed him ten dollars. He rolled the note between his fingers.

'You'll have to hide it', I warned.

He spat out phlegm. 'I have places Mom will never find'.

I gazed at my blood in the snow.

'Like candyfloss', I said out loud to no one.

The Secret Life of Madame Defarge

During the French Revolution people still expected love to save them. Or failing that, some brand of loyalty inbred from friend to friend, servant to kind master, lover to lover, man to God. They expected love or loyalty at every last moment, at every last second just before the guillotine's blade sliced its way through their necks. How many called for God then or at least for someone to miraculously save them? A hand of God or an angel's wing? It was the fear that killed most of them before the blade did. That gut-sick fear of watching your own feet walk to your death. The buckles on your shoes that used to glint now shone up the shit and blood and the stink from your own person and the grinning spit smeared on the mob's faces.

If you were to ask anyone of those that faced their death that way, they would say something similar ... how the faces of the crowd crept into each other. How the laughter and the seething hunger for blood and the sound of neck bones snapping was echoed in the chittering of the mob's teeth, as if small carnivorous insects had crawled from separate tongues and set up an orchestra of death and hate.

And Madame Defarge seemed no different, although she did not exist in anything other than an ancient novel, she existed well enough on the sidelines of the guillotine as she knitted away the lives of the filthy aristocracy. Her breasts puffed over the frilled neckline of her new dress which she had been careful to raise above the blood and the crowd's spit and urine.

Her friend Rosa sat next to her underneath the guillotine. Rosa was easily bored and was tired of waiting. She had a lover, she said. Big with muscled arms that her fingers could not get around. She tapped her foot, looked this way and that, then winked at Madame Defarge.

'Eh, Therese, do you want to know his name?'

Madame Defarge ignored her. She was also bored, but hid it under her smile. Rosa said nothing else, but her eyes stayed too long on Madame Defarge's face

'He's a good lover, Therese', she said, eventually.

Madame Defarge shrugged. She decided to say nothing.

'But he says things in his dreams', Rosa added.

Madame Defarge leaned forward and gazed at the far edge of the crowd. There were dark birds in the sky waiting for blood and meat. Madame Defarge grunted a little. She had loved the guillotine for months, but death was rampant now. Aristocracy had to be erased. Priests and nuns also … those who insisted that all of this was against God's order must be put to death in the same way … but they were killing others too. People who asked questions, people who read the books priests had read, people who wondered why the leaders of the Revolution still looked richer than others, people who said maybe Robespierre was getting a little too big for his boots. Even Madame Defarge, with her new petticoats and her fancy walk, well ... no wonder people sometimes look at you, Rosa had mentioned once.

Madame Defarge focussed on her knitting. She had lost count of all the names and now she just used colours. Red, white, green, and the colours of the rich, magenta, aubergines, crimson, burnt sienna like mustard on an aristo's dinner plate and blue like the hottest sky – the sort of blue that seemed to reach inside your lungs and make breathing a hard pleasure.

These were the things that made Madame Defarge uneasy these days. Death could not satisfy her. It stank, it dirtied her new clothes, clothes that she had tried to hide in the beginning but Rosa had noticed, Rosa with her quick, insect eyes and plucking fingers. Rosa who had joked, 'Therese Defarge has aristo bones hidden beneath her skin'. Rosa whose nails smelled of ingrained shit from wiping her own arse with her fingers. Rosa who had not changed. Rosa who had not kept up with her best friend, but Rosa had not needed to.

'His name is Ernst ... like your husband', Rosa whispered.

Madame Defarge felt a terrible fear finger the edges of her heart. Something she had suspected, yet never dared take as truth. Her husband inside Rosa's thighs. She smiled and said nothing. She wound some wool around her finger and readied it for the needle. She glanced up at the congregating birds that fluffed out their wings, picked fleas with their beaks and looked back at her with dead, black eyes.

Madame Defarge plucked at the neckline of her dress to cover her breasts from the sudden chill. A man in the crowd caught her eyes and licked his lips.

'Here they come', Rosa sang.

In the beginning Madame Defarge had relished the guillotine. It suited her grief to have a blood lust underlying her sorrow. It made her get up in the mornings. It made her sell wine and march each day to the Place de la Révolution to cheer on the executions. It made the memory of her son settle in her heart. His soft black hair and his green eyes, his mouth on her breast when he was a baby and his thin, narrow chest against her stomach when he was older and still not man enough to ignore her.

Oh, Madame Defarge knew love. She knew how it had burned in her grief and had turned into a hot hate and at night in her husband's arms, she pleaded with him to fuck her so that a new child would grow. She even prayed to God to make her husband someone who could save her in this way. She had watched Ernst's teeth tear meat from chicken bones, watched his tongue fight its way through gristle and fat and she had longed for his teeth and tongue.

He did not kiss her anymore. After their son's death, Ernst Defarge had remained quiet. His eyes said nothing. Madame Defarge thought of her son, soft and warm against her and his breath bubbling at her breasts. She thought of her husband covering himself up. She thought of Rosa opening her legs. Rosa, whose belly had never grown full no matter how many men got inside her.

Madame Defarge pressed her fists into her stomach. She closed her eyes and imagined that she was a different woman. Someone Ernst would love. Someone he would never expect to discover in his old wife's kitchen or in their bedroom in the dead, secret night when she whispered her craving to him. She had tried to be any kind of woman to him. He liked them gentle, she knew. Soft and sweet like birds with velvet breasts.

Rosa was smaller. Rosa had fairer skin and thin wrists and a body that looked too much like a child's. She leaned forward like a child to watch the tumbrel as it made its way to the guillotine's steps.

Madame Defarge shifted within her own large hips and noticed how her new dress stretched tight across her knees. It smelled of roses and lavender. The woman who had worn it before her had been smaller; delicate arms and breasts with thin collarbones under white skin. Perhaps she had listened to poetry under lamplight with the sour smell of wine in a glass beside her fingers; pretty fingers, small like those of a porcelain doll.

Or perhaps she looked like the young girl who had now stepped from the tumbrel. Madame Defarge stopped knitting. She stared as the girl was pushed forward. She waited until the girl drew level, then Madame Defarge reached out with one knitting needle and tapped the girl's forearm. The girl turned like a broken doll turns on its final hinge and she smiled at Madame Defarge. The girl's face was swollen. Her teeth were crushed and her bottom lip had been torn. Madame Defarge murmured at the girl as you would at a frightened kitten.

For all those seconds that she stared and smiled at the girl, Madame Defarge wanted many things. She wanted this girl's once lovely face and body. She wanted the sound the air would have made as this girl would have danced through it all those times before. Madame Defarge longed for the smell of perfumed candles and goose hearts in jelly. She longed for a gilt bed and bread as white as clouds.

Yet at the edge of her longing there was a sound that Madame Defarge recognised. It was the crowd's silence. It breathed in against her …

'Kill the bitch', Madame Defarge screamed. She jabbed her needles into the girl's arm and thrust her face close to the girl's destroyed mouth, then she spat hard.

'Kill the bitch', she screamed again.

Her knitting group took up the chant. Their needles clacked in time. 'Kill the bitch', 'kill the bitch', 'kill the bitch'.

The girl was lifted by her elbows and Madame Defarge crowed with joy. Her blood-lust blackened the inside of her mind, so that she thought and smelled nothing else but the hot iron odour of blood. The mob joined in Madame's scream for death. Their eyes swivelled from watching the girl being positioned at the edge of the guillotine, to the woman roaring into the air and stabbing her needles into the sun.

'Kill the bitch. Kill the little whore', Madame Defarge screamed.

'Kill the bitch. Kill the whore', the mob ranted.

The stench and sticky thrill of blood made the mob sniff death like a lover. The girl's beauty was exaggerated against the executioner's bulk and the sun caught the line of her limbs through her shift. Madame Defarge glanced over the crowd. She could not see her husband, but she knew his face would have the same look that was on every other man's face. The girl was laid on the board and then slid forward, so that her head and neck hung over the waiting basket. The mob silenced. The girl's lips were moving.

Out of nowhere, Madame Defarge cried out, 'What's your name? What's your name?'

'Who cares?' said Rosa and elbowed Madame Defarge into silence before smiling up at the girl. 'Bye, bye, Pretty', Rosa called, 'Don't forget your prayers, little bird. Don't forget to fly away when your head is gone!'

The girl stared down at Madame Defarge who held up her hands as if to pluck the girl from her death. The girl was praying so hard now that her vision had melted the crowd into a dark sea that murmured like a lullaby.

Madame Defarge saw the blade and stuck out her fingers to stop it. She wanted a name. She thought – a new name instead of Therese and a new dress, a new perfume. A new woman for Ernst. A new child.

'Tell me your name', she screamed right into the heart of the mob's silence.

The girl's head dropped into the basket.

The mob cheered. The girl's head was lifted. It looked too small to be real. Madame Defarge gazed at it. No name, she realised. No name.

'Like a pretty plum', Rosa laughed. 'Eh, Therese? Plopped like a pretty plum'. She poked her knitting needles into Madame Defarge's new dress, paused, then stepped closer to Madame Defarge's ear and whispered, 'You are in the way, Therese'.

Madame Defarge stepped back. Her knitting had fallen into the slime underfoot. The birds had settled down to eating. The sky was still blue and hard. Ernst was either in the tavern or waiting for Rosa. Madame Defarge sat down on her bench. She was tired. The guillotine thudded down on the necks of the remaining prisoners and Madame Defarge stopped counting after a while.

New Bodies for Old

David heard the 'ssh-ssh' of Fiona's deodorant spray and knew she was almost ready. She was supposed to be an actress and had acted in college. She acted still. She pounced on bit parts in the drama workshops that littered Galway. She had her dream and she wanted her big break. Something to get her out of the actual shit of her life, although David had told her and had made a compliment of it, that she was good at this and she was good at him.

David came from Galway and had no one to lie to. Fiona came from Cork and chose Galway for its art life. She believed in God. 'I pray like a Russian', she mentioned when drunk. She believed in sex, in the life her bargain with David afforded her and she believed in her dream.

She also believed that David was like any other man. He liked games. He liked fucking and he enjoyed treats. All kinds of treats and, naturally, he paid more. Always that little bit more for that little bit extra. But he was bored now.

So David began to find others in street corners or in pubs. Men and women whose bodies had an exciting, hard and grimy feel. Bodies that fed a need in David to be someone else, someone of substance and secrets.

Five years ago, Fiona had seemed like an answer. He had first seen her smoking outside the Town Hall during a play's intermission. When friends called her name, she waved them on, preferring to look at David. It was a look that nailed him. She walked up to him and said, 'I'm an actress. You?'

'Business man'.

'Enjoying the play?'

'Can't stand it'.

She smiled at him. 'It's supposed to be atmospheric, display inner conflict and promise redemption'.

'Oh', he said.

They struck the bargain because she expected money and he liked paying for her. Her body was thin and adaptable. Sometimes she seemed like a boy with a tight narrow walk and other times she spread like a woman, hips wide, and she could laugh, hardly ever girlish, but sexy and promising everything.

David had never expected to grow used to Fiona. He had presumed that her acting would guard against that, that she would continue to fascinate him with her characters, her voice, and he played along. He told her that he could lose himself inside her. She laughed, held up her arms and said she was only skin, just skin to put on other people. 'And on stage', she said, 'on stage'.

David thought five years was a long time.

Fiona entered the room. She looked young. Her hair was blonde and fastened into curls. She wore a red pleated skirt with a narrow white shirt which she began to unbutton. She glanced at David, then re-did them.

'I'm tired', she announced.

David didn't respond.

Fiona sat on the carpet before his feet and fanned out her skirt across her thighs. A pair of old-fashioned spectacles peeped from her shirt pocket and her fingers were ink-stained.

'But I've made an effort', she said.

'As what?' David said.

'Semi-school girl', Fiona answered, 'Lolita with brains'.

'I want something else', David said.

'I told you, I'm tired. Consider this the best you're going to get tonight. Give me another week and I'll think of something else'.

'You're not that good anymore, Fiona'.

Fiona bent her head forward with a dramatic sigh. 'Christ, what a little prick you can be'. She looked at him. 'Drink then?'

'Fine', he said.

Fiona stretched upwards to pluck an almost empty whiskey bottle from the fireplace mantelpiece. She held it under the room's light and shook it.

'It's cloudy', she remarked. 'Something must have got into it. Dust, probably'. She found two glasses and poured out their drinks. She drank fast.

'You're not touching yours', she said to David.

'Don't need it', he said.

Fiona poured another drink. David watched her. There were shadows under her eyes and a cold sore on her mouth, half-concealed by lipstick.

'I want to see you naked', he told her.

Fiona shrugged. 'You usually do'.

'Just tonight', he said.

She stared at him. He lit a cigarette and stared at her bare toes. Her toe-nails had an old yellow tinge. He flicked ash onto the carpet and waited.

Fiona stood up. She unbuttoned her blouse and dropped her skirt. She lifted one foot, then another, as she yanked off her underwear. Her blouse and spectacles dropped to the floor.

'Look', she said.

He looked. He looked at a pale body going to fat at the shoulder blades and waist. He stubbed out his cigarette and said nothing for long seconds. Fiona put her clothes back on. She took a cigarette from his packet, lit it, then sat back down with her drink.

'You've found someone else', she said.

He said nothing.

Fiona smiled and practised wearing the spectacles. 'I've a job. I must have forgotten to tell you'.

'Acting', he said.

She smiled. 'Yeah, that's right. In one of those old Irish plays Americans love. It'll do well in the festival. I'll be busy'.

'Getting your face known', he said.

'Exactly'.

David lit another cigarette. He supposed that there always was some kind of ritual to saying goodbye, yet he said nothing and she said nothing, and, as he left her, she remained near the fireplace, looking at something else.

TWO VAMPIRES

Two vampires cross the road, enter a café and order eggs. The shorter vampire has a tight, thin face with almost yellow eyes. His name is Robert and he is Welsh. He is one-hundred-years-old and prefers French sixties clothes.

His companion, Francis, is taller and darker. He was originally thirty-two-years-old some twenty years ago and had been an architect. His premature grey hair has a little black through it, and the last human thing he remembers is his wife calling to him.

While the two vampires await their eggs, they study the café's clientele, which is mainly young since the school day has just ended. Francis is not interested in them, but in the small, thin, blonde waitress who has taken their order. Robert also watches her. His face has stiffened as it always does when he sees prey. After some seconds he nods and nonchalantly wets his fingertips; trails sugar across them, then sucks each one clean.

Francis places the sugar dispenser out of reach, sits into his corner seat and lays his head back, as if tired. He listens to the sounds around him. It is a habit and in the café's light and in the stretch of his body he is aware of how normal he appears.

Robert, however, is anxious. He is disturbed by humans and only considers them food. When he kills them, he hides their faces with his hand, shutting off their eyes and their mouths. Francis says it's because Robert must still remember how things had been – how things had once felt – but Francis is a romantic and still believes in such things.

Robert loves the death he forces into humans. He loves how their skin tears under his teeth and their attempts at screaming turn to nothing in his ears. He has stopped remembering anything of his life before, yet in the beginning, like Francis, he presumed he could not forget. He had expected to remember how the smell of fresh bread filled a morning or how he always longed to be clean ... but he forgot it all.

Now he appreciates the distance between him and humans. Their lives are alien, only their blood means anything. Robert had once tried to explain it to Francis who did not listen, not because he was not interested, but because his hatred for Robert – although finally vague after all these years together – remained inside him still.

And Robert cannot explain. Not really, and not with any real care. Instead he accepts two things. Humans are food and Francis is beautiful – a vampire Robert believes he himself should have been – with a long, lazy naturalism in his body and rapid eyes to choose prey, in spite of the fact that blood is almost wasted on Francis. His hatred for Robert has seen to that.

Francis understands that blood means survival and he cannot consider his life without it, otherwise there is only starvation, a slow desiccation of skin and bones. Since his soul is gone, he believes so might he be, and that is why he insists on remembering and coaxing the hate into his heart. It keeps him as himself.

Yet they have remained together. There is no answer for that and neither of them mentions it, and through the years they have developed a natural rhythm in their dead lives, culminating in one necessary ritual.

Every so often, they share a victim.

They take turns to choose and kill. Robert is invariably quick; hand over face and teeth in neck. When he kills, he knows Francis is resentful. Francis likes to hear their voices, likes to watch their faces. That's his romance and he has never lost it.

Francis has opened his eyes and now watches the waitress approach the table. He can smell the fat-grease that has spattered her apron. Curls show from beneath her cap, and on each palm she balances their plate of eggs. She is aware of Francis's gaze as she places knives and forks on either side of each plate.

Francis smiles at her and she returns it. Her smile makes her look younger.

'Coffee's on its way', she tells them and retreats.

'You'll frighten her away', warns Robert.

'I won't', Francis promises.

Robert plunges his knife into his eggs. With one finger, he cleans up the yolk dribble, then licks it. His eyes fasten on Francis who cuts his eggs into strips before eating them.

'Why not one of those school-kids?' Robert demands. 'You can pick one off easy. They don't always travel home in packs'.

Francis shrugs and does not need to answer. Robert knows he should be used to it all by now. Whenever it is Francis's turn, a woman is always chosen.

Robert studies the waitress. What he can remember of women is very little. In his time as a human, they were as desperate as he. They littered the streets and perhaps he fucked some, but he soon forgot the sound and smell of them.

The waitress returns with coffee. Robert looks at her neck as she pours. He avoids her face. Her neck is freckled, dainty and ageing. He sees where he would shove her throat back with the heel of his hand if she were his choice.

She mentions the weather to Francis and her right ankle bends sideways like a young girl, delighted and shy, and not the tired woman she is. Robert looks at Francis's face and his stomach constricts when he sees that Francis's gaze on the woman is clear and has that strange beauty. Beneath his eyes, the skin is dark as if he could still have his own blood there, warm and human-like.

Francis points to the waitress's apron.

'Oh Jesus ... this', she flaps it out from her dress. 'The cook's sick and I got roped in'.

Francis sips his coffee, then slots his long hands one into the other over his cup. He smiles at her and she nods at their plates.

'I cooked your eggs'.

Robert snaps at her. 'We know'.

Francis ignores him. He's examining the woman's face. She has pale skin with light freckles. Her eyes are brown and narrow. Nothing like his wife. Nothing like her face which still comes to him, even if he has to claw its memory back; and her smell had been nothing like grease. Yet her exact smell left him long ago, and the smells of the women he kills now are only approximations.

Some women are clean. Others are stale with perfume, while others smell of sweat or merely of themselves. Those are the ones he prefers. He wants to remember that his wife smelt like herself when he had left her that morning and also that she had smiled at him, and if there had been a kiss, he can still imagine it.

Francis says something that never fails. 'You have a beautiful smile'.

The waitress is pleased. She curls her notepad in her hand.

'Would you like something else?'

'What's your name?'

'Lillian'.

Francis smiles. 'Old-fashioned'.

'My grandmother's. I wasn't baptised with it. That's a different name. But I was given "Lillian". She made sure of that'.

Lillian holds up her pencil. 'Anything else?'

'More coffee', Francis replies.

Lillian pours more coffee into his cup, then swings the pot towards Robert who stands up fast and silent. He slits his eyes at her and she almost yelps in fear. She steps back, gathers up her smile and says, 'I'm in your way ... sorry'.

Robert looks at Francis. 'I'll be outside'.

Lillian watches him go. 'Is he alright?'

'He's fine. He just wants cold air'.

Francis indicates to Lillian to sit. She checks that none of the other staff are watching, then sits in Robert's seat.

Francis leans in and Lillian gets shy.

'Lillian'.

'Yes?'

'How is it that you are here?'

Francis calculates that she will think this an unusual opening, and he has picked its deliberate phrasing because she has a smell about her now, not the grease, since her apron is hidden under the table, but a sullen odour of heavy perfume on her blouse. Francis has learned that women who want more in life use perfumes of that kind.

Kitchen sweat has made Lillian's face gleam and about her are the sounds of the café. Clacking cutlery, the drift and soar of voices, eating and the swing of the entrance doors collect about her and become as real as they had ever been to Francis.

'It's just a job', she replies. She also leans forward and uses one finger to pull a curl from above her ear. 'It's a stop-gap. I have plans'. She glances up and notices Robert standing on the path outside, his back to the café window.

'Is he okay?'

Francis reclaims her attention. 'What plans, Lillian?'

'Oh, you know. Get out of here. Get a new life'.

'Specifically', Francis says, and at her frown, 'I mean exactly what sort of plans? How do you plan to live a new life?'

Lillian lowers her voice. 'I plan to be an archaeologist'.

Francis expects this to be a lie. In a greasy-spoon café, in a dump of a town like this, to want to be an archaeologist is ridiculous.

'It's a good plan', Francis tells her.

She nods. 'Always loved history and old things ... I used to dig up the back garden ... found loads of crap'.

Her eyes shine and inside Francis's cold skin and behind his bones, he is sure something stirs.

'When do you finish work, Lillian?'

Lillian pinches her fingers as she considers. 'Half-an-hour'.

He nods. 'We can meet outside'.

'Yeah ... sure. Yeah, that's fine'.

'An archaeologist', he compliments her.

She slips out of her seat and she smoothes her apron across her stomach. Someone yells her name and she flicks a smile at Francis before getting back to her job.

Francis continues to drink his coffee. He does not need to glance at the window to know that Robert is still standing outside, nursing his suffering and his hunger. Francis knows that Robert will always wait, will continue with this ritual because Francis desires his revenge this way; because Francis's own hate will not allow him to continue his dead life alone, and because until the day Robert made Francis a vampire, Robert had always been lonely.

It had happened on a hot Saturday afternoon and perhaps he had been working overtime or maybe he had been shopping, but Francis had rung his wife. He had listened to her voice until there was an instant pain and a long pull on his blood as if the whole of him was being dragged away. Robert had him.

From that moment on, Francis fed on two things; blood and his frustrated hate for Robert. This hate has made his heart live inside him. He kills people, desperate to be a part of them, whole and real again, but there is only Robert with his skinny face, his accent and his loneliness so powerful that it is like a smell Francis cannot escape from.

Francis leaves a tip beside his cup and makes his way over to pay his bill. Another waitress, spotty and disinterested takes his money. Lillian catches Francis's eye and he nods at her. She watches him exit the café and join up with Robert. They talk for a few seconds then Robert walks off.

When Lillian finishes work, she finds Francis waiting by a car. She gives him a smile and they walk on to a pub.

'Where's your friend?' Lillian asks.

'Found something to do', Francis answers.

Inside the pub there is only the landlady who stands up from a seat behind the bar and greets them.

'Monday night', says Lillian.

She sits and takes a packet of cigarettes from her coat pocket. Francis refuses her offer, and while Lillian lights up, he gives their order to the landlady.

Lillian smokes and watches Francis. She flicks ash onto the floor.

'You seem nice', she tells him. She inhales, looks him down and then up. 'I like meeting men like you'.

'Often?'

'Sometimes'.

There is a cough in the darkness beyond their alcove and Lillian swivels to see the landlady placing their drinks on the bar counter. Francis collects them.

'I like your hands', Lillian says, then takes one fast gulp of her drink.

'Really?' Francis turns his right palm up and Lillian touches it.

'Long', she says. 'Thin ... artistic'.

Francis drinks and listens. He likes to talk with women he has decided to kill, and he prefers to disregard their normal expectation of a quick fuck after a session of alcohol. Instead he studies their faces and tries to remember his wife.

Sometimes these women speak of sadness, of lives ruined by death or mistakes, or the children they shouldn't really have had, or those jobs that swallowed them whole.

With each conversation, Francis understands that he is seeing lives he will never possess, only destroy, and because of this, he never thinks beyond his victim's death or the consequences for whatever lives they leave behind.

He is like Robert in this respect. When the blood is drunk and the body left, there is only the fact that their small ritual has ended, until the next time, and they return to their usual hunt.

'You're an artist', Lillian insists.

'Yes', Francis lies.

'What kind?'

'Sculpture', he tells her.

She smiles and inside Francis there is a mixture of hunger for her blood and hunger for what her smile may mean. She takes his hand and touches the veins on the back of his hand.

'I love beautiful hands. You know, people warn you about faces, never about hands ... ' She drops his hand and raises her empty glass. 'I'd like another'. She glances about for the landlady.

'You're a fast drunk', Francis observes.

'I need to be', she says. 'No ... let her bring them. You stay here'. She taps her fingers on the table. 'They warn you about everything else ...' she jerks her attention to the drinks the landlady is placing on the table.

'I'll be busy out the back for a while', the woman says to Francis. 'If you want any more, you'll have to shout'.

She returns to the bar and puts Francis's money into the till before disappearing into the back.

'I drink too much', Lillian is saying. Francis keeps looking at her. Lillian shrugs. 'All because I love beautiful hands like yours'.

Lillian yawns and does not notice Robert move out from the darkness. Francis glances at the bar. Empty. Robert is trembling for blood, but waits. Francis whispers something and Lillian puts down her glass.

'Sorry?' she says.

Francis whispers again and Lillian frowns. Francis leans forward so that Lillian's face is near his, and he is near to her eyes, and abruptly his wife is as beautiful as she always was. He says her name.

'Anna?' Lillian says. 'That's not my name'. She draws on her cigarette, then swirls the last ice cubes in her drink. 'We don't have to play guessing games. It wasn't "Anna". It was "Imelda" ... thick, dumpy "Imelda" after some dead aunt'.

Lillian stops smoking once she realises that Francis is just staring at her, no motion in his face and she becomes aware of something behind her.

Robert coughs and nods a greeting at the bright alarm in Lillian's face, who turns back to Francis and smiles fast, pleading with her eyes and voice. 'He's come back. Make him leave'.

'He doesn't hear you', Robert tells her.

'Of course he hears me', she says. 'Francis', she says. She taps on one of his fingers.

Robert steps closer. He touches Lillian's curls. They are like silk rotted into string.

'Francis doesn't see you', he tells her.

Lillian half-laughs despite the slow grease of fear in her lungs and she clicks her fingers in Francis's face.

'Is it epilepsy?' she whispers.

'Sort of', Robert says. He uses one hand to stroke the jagged side-split in Lillian's hair and he can hear his effect on her breath. He relishes the ratchet of fear in the muscles of her throat.

'Kiss him', he whispers.

Lillian refuses, but Robert shoves her forward. Her breath shoots up into Francis's face. He gulps it in and pain opens up inside him. Robert looks at Francis and sees what has always terrified him – all Francis's worn beauty – almost alive, almost singing with blood inside him.

'Jesus', cries Lillian.

She tries to fight, but Robert grips her. She screams and Francis lunges. His teeth gouge her neck and her very last breath is stopped by Robert's hand.

Together they take her outside and find a hiding place where Robert drinks his fill and, when he is finished, they fold the body into a nearby rubbish skip. They say nothing to each other. Francis never speaks of what he remembers, and Robert has learned not to ask.

Instead, Robert plays 'pat-a-cake' fingers on the steering wheel and he can feel the numb pain glow in his knuckles and his blood keeps warm for seconds longer, but the cold night outside goes dark and darker and slowly there is nothing left.

Journey Back

Marie considered ignoring the priest who would not move off the veranda.

'I've come to get you', he said. 'We'll travel in the Land Rover. An hour, give or take'. He squinted and slapped dead a fly on the veranda post.

'You have to go', he insisted.

'Will he survive?' Marie asked.

'He's waiting', replied the priest, then stuck his fingers into the carved figures of her new rosewood table. He sucked his teeth as he admired the surface, curving his hand against its rim.

'Those Hausa fellows were around so', he said.

'Yes', she said.

'Like coming here, don't they?'

Marie rubbed her bare feet backward and forward on the veranda floor. She loathed Fr Timothy. His large face and slit eyes always noticed things that sniffed of confession. She stood up and brushed her new, bright-flowered dress, then padded over to where she had left her sandals.

'That's good. That's good', said Fr Timothy.

Marie half-rested against a veranda chair as she fastened each sandal. Her lungs hurt beneath her dress's bodice and she knew that before evening came, it would be grimy with sweat. She used tissues from her bag to pat her face dry as she walked across the small dirt compound to the waiting Land Rover and sat in. She rolled down the window and wanted to cry.

The priest told the story. A bloody huge latrine and the boys in the sixth-form class had been roped into digging along with her husband. Of course, he knew how to organise them. Got them their shovels and got them into a rhythm.

'Right', Marie said.

She was damned if she was going to play the role of loving wife. She licked sweat from her upper lip and inched her hips further away from Fr Timothy's shadow on the seat beside her. She should have left before this. Forgot her husband, forgot the church, and forgot Africa. She should have made her way to America to become someone else.

'He loves his work', said Fr Timothy, and continued with the story. A big, blasted hole, her husband at the bottom with two school boys. Her husband climbed out and thought things were safe. Two minutes later, the hole collapsed and buried the boys.

'They couldn't be bothered to help us try to save them. Life is dirt-cheap here. But now they say it's our fault. "Fucking white devils", they called us'.

Marie said nothing and gazed across the bush landscape. The hottest place next to hell, some well-meaning English ex-pat had told her at the club one night. He was a tall, gentle-faced man despite his heavy skin and drunken hands. Never mind, she had thought, and allowed his hands pluck at the waistband of her skirt. She forgot his name soon enough. Forgot how he smelled when they half-wrestled against an outside wall, forgot how she was supposed to play the game –

just pretend it didn't happen. Add yourself to the rumour mill and if you perfect the ex-colonial accent, you'll fit in just fine.

Her husband never listened to rumours. Instead he hit her. Once, even twice, she was prepared to forgive and she had the confession line down pat. Father, forgive me, I know everything I do. Somehow, even with that line, she could have wrangled forgiveness. You can wrangle almost anything, another lover told her once.

She remembered his hands most of all. Long, beautiful fingers held up towards a hotel room ceiling – and God, she loved what those fingers could do to her. She had fashioned a whole love from those fingers. They kept her alive, made her feel flesh and blood, and not just the punch-bag wife reflected in the bathroom mirror.

That lover had wanted to save her and, most times, she was tempted to agree. Yes, I'll love you. I'll be the most glorious woman for you. I'll bring all my sin and beauty right to your door.

The fairy tale never worked, but even with him gone she could still call up the image of his fingers onto her own and imagine how it might have been possible.

Marie steadied herself as the Land Rover bumped its way into the police compound and drew up to the office headquarters. She got out and looked around for the baying mob, but there was nothing but the heat and sound of laughter from the cook's kitchen.

Fr Timothy lounged against the Land Rover and jerked his head at the police commissioner's door. Marie patted at the creases in her skirt and went inside. She smiled at the officer behind the reception desk and saw her husband's shadow move behind the frosted glass of the commissioner's office. He and the commissioner were laughing.

Marie sat on the low, brown bench and wished with all her heart that there was nothing left. Nothing of him and nothing of her. Fr Timothy came to the door and smiled.

'Soon have the pair of you back home', he said.

Sweet Frankie

Frankie's daddy always promised he'd be where he said he would be. I'll see you in five minutes, half-an-hour, this afternoon, or when your mother gets home. Frankie was five years old when he realised other children weren't really hit as much. He kept his mouth shut after too many questions. His teacher, very pretty, very sweet and who also smelled lovely, called him into her office. She gave him two lollipops and he wanted to sit on her knee. He didn't understand the questions she asked him.

'Do you love your mammy and daddy?'

He nodded.

'Do your mammy and daddy love you?'

He nodded again.

'Do they get really angry sometimes?'

Frankie sucked hard on his lollipop. Oh, you really like sweets his teacher said, but she looked worried. She bit into her pencil and opened and closed a notebook on her desk. She took the pencil out of her mouth and tried to hum a song. Frankie filled in the words, but he kept his voice very quiet, just in case she got angry.

Frankie liked to sing. He liked how big it made him feel. Sometimes he roared songs out of him, but always with the pillow in his mouth. Frankie drummed his shoes against the chair he was sitting on. He was getting a little afraid and now he didn't like his teacher anymore. Her smile was all wrong and he didn't believe her when she said if he went out to play now, things would be okay.

That's what she said. Things would be okay now. He made himself repeat it throughout the whole day. He didn't play football in case he forgot the words. He hardly spoke to anyone. He ate his lunch alone and fed some of his sandwich to the ants that crawled across the green wooden table. He screwed his eyes up when he looked at the sun and he remembered how his mammy said he would have to ask the nurse to put sunscreen on him.

Frankie put his other sandwich back into his lunch box and went to the sick-room. The nurse had a special smile just for him. He handed her the sun-screen and he stood just exactly as he always did when his mammy put it on him. The nurse had different hands and they smelled funny. Her hands were peeling. Frankie saw tiny bits of skin dangling from her fingers and palms. The nurse upended the bottle into one hand and pounded on the end of the bottle with her other hand. She asked questions as well.

'So how are you today, Frankie?'

Frankie shrugged his shoulders and winced at the coldness of the sun lotion. The nurse patted her hands over his arm, smiled into his face and then very gently turned his arm this way and that. She did the same to his other arm. Then she crouched down and did the same to his legs, only this time she had to skid a little on her heels to get behind his knees.

'Christ', she said as if something had hurt her.

He started and she put her fingers on his elbow.

'It's okay, Frankie. Just looking at this cut here. Can't let the lotion get into it because it could sting and make you cry. How did you get that nasty cut?'

His mammy had forgotten to put the plaster on because she had been crying and her face was covered in blisters and Frankie had said nothing; just eaten his cornflakes, drunk his chocolate milk, got his bag and waited outside for his daddy to come out the front door with the car keys and his big voice.

'Come on, Frankie. Time for school'.

In the backseat, Frankie watched the sweat drip onto his daddy's shirt collar. After a while his daddy pulled at his collar, then undid his tie. Now and again, Frankie could see his daddy look at him in the mirror.

'Okay, Frankie?'

'Okay', said Frankie.

'What are you going to learn today, Frankie?'

'What the teacher says'.

'That's good', his daddy said. His daddy's eyes flicked and swerved to watch the road. Frankie felt his stomach follow the corners after the car. He has never told his mammy that the car makes him sick. It makes a special hot water come up into his mouth and once Frankie did let it come out, but never again. That's what his daddy said – never again – and he slung his hand hard across Frankie's head so that colours shot into Frankie's eyes and the last bit of his sick bubbled down his shirt.

He didn't go to school that day. His father turned the car around and told Frankie to go into his mother and get her to wash his shirt.

'I'll be back in the afternoon. We'll do extra homework to make up', his daddy said.

Frankie loved his mammy very much. She had red hair that she curled around her fingers as she cooked the meals and she always made sure that Frankie stayed quiet when he was at the table. Frankie knew that already without being told, but his mammy never stopped telling him that it was important.

Frankie was five years old and very sweet. His mammy told him that. Even Mrs Feeney who ran the shop down the street thought so. She'd bend down whenever she saw him, say 'Choose, Sweet Frankie!' and she'd hold her fists out. Frankie never chose wrong, because Mrs Feeney always hid sweets in both fists. She'd ruffle his hair, stand up, and if Frankie looked up at her sometimes, instead of the sweets, he would see Mrs Feeney's face change when she said something to his mammy.

'How are you, Anne?'

'Fine, fine', his mammy would say and move over to the shop counter. 'Frankie, go over there and have a look at the comics and eat your sweets. Did you thank Mrs Feeney?'

'Thanks, Mrs Feeney'.

Frankie loved *The Incredible Hulk*. The Hulk was big and green and could crush people if he wanted to. He smashed cars then changed back into being normal. And no one knew who he really was. No one knew what he could magic into.

Frankie sat on the ground, ate his sweets and read a comic. Sometimes Mrs Feeney gave him a free one. Not all the time. Only when his mammy had a long talk and if Mrs Feeney looked like she had cried. Then she was extra kind. Then she would bend down and kiss Frankie on the cheek and say what a sweet, lovely boy he was and wouldn't he always watch out for his mammy?

Frankie couldn't always do that.

Sometimes he'd be too tired and fall asleep, only to wake up and hear his mammy screaming. He'd hear her being slammed into things and he knew not to get out of bed because she didn't want that. The last time he had got out of bed to help her, she had yelled at him to go back to his room and his daddy stood there with his mammy's hair in his fists, because he was holding her head up and she looked like a doll.

Other times, Frankie's daddy would come back when he said he would and he'd be kind. He'd bring back something nice like flowers and chocolates and they'd all eat them instead of dinner. Afterwards they'd watch something on the television and then Frankie would be told to go to bed and later there'd be no sound. Nothing at all.

Frankie's daddy believed in turning up when he said he would. Frankie learned that from him. Frankie learned that it was good manners to smile, look tidy and turn up when you were supposed to. Frankie never finished all of his food on his plate and sometimes he only cut off a little with his knife, then put it onto his fork and that was all he would eat. His daddy said Frankie would get hungry soon enough.

Frankie began to feed the birds as well as the ants. He preferred birds and he knew The Hulk could be very kind to baby things, so Frankie was too. He didn't like the noise of the playground and so he just sat with the birds.

It was his daddy's belt-buckle that had made the cut on the back of Frankie's knee. His daddy put his mammy's head under the hot tap in the kitchen and shoved his body against her legs to make her stop kicking. Frankie heard her scream – first water, then her scream, then a funny mixture of them both, like she was singing bubbles.

Frankie tried to save his mammy. He ran into his daddy's legs and bit them. He bit enough to feel the blood come through his daddy's trousers and into his mouth. His daddy tried to shake Frankie off, but Frankie bit harder. Frankie felt his chest grow bigger as if something was trying to get out of him. He bit and bit and bit. His daddy's hands tried to pull Frankie's head off, but Frankie imagined how The Hulk would never let go so neither would he.

His daddy got his fingers into the sides of Frankie's mouth and prised Frankie's jaws apart. Frankie remembered later on how there was just silence in the room until his daddy struggled to stand and then went out of the room.

'Wait there', his daddy said. 'I'll be back in a minute'.

Frankie stood with blood dribbling down his chin. He looked at his mammy who was crying with no sound. Her face was pressed against the sink cupboard. It was red and bashed and she tried to cover it with her hair.

Frankie could hear his daddy coming back down the hall, so Frankie swallowed the blood in his mouth. He wanted to run, but his mammy was crying. His daddy came into the kitchen with his belt wrapped over his fist.

'This is what you get', his daddy said.

The nurse put a plaster on the cut and made a phone call. She spoke for a long time and now and again she smiled over at Frankie. When she finished talking into the phone, she asked him if he would like a juice and he said he'd like an orange one.

'Look what I also have for you, Frankie'.

She gave him a piece of chocolate and also some pens to colour in a picture book. After a while, Frankie's teacher came in to see the nurse, but she smiled at Frankie first. She said his daddy was here to take him home. Frankie put down his pens and the last square of chocolate, but the nurse said he could eat that up. Before he went out the door, the nurse crouched down and looked into his eyes and said:

'You know, Frankie, you shouldn't be getting those kinds of cuts at all'.

Frankie nodded and the nurse stood up and gave him a red lollipop from a pile of lollipops on a shelf. Then his teacher brought him out to his daddy who was sitting on the long low bench outside the staff room. His daddy was smiling and took Frankie by the hand and told him to say goodbye to his teacher.

'Goodnight, Miss Hanlon'.

'Goodnight, Mr Folan. Goodnight, Frankie'.

Frankie smiled at his teacher. Sometimes he imagined her calling him Sweet Frankie as well.

Sweat and Feet

Everything about Jon was clean, whereas Susanne attracted dirt. It was in her nature. She loved summer for its hot, grubby moments and its people smell. She never tired of watching her own sweat gather like a second skin on her arms, and in the late afternoons, in her room and on her own, she'd lie naked on her bed, feeling her sweat cool into salt.

Susanne noticed Jon's feet when she and two friends decided to ditch work and spend the afternoon at the beach. Susanne wore her favourite swimsuit which was tight about her breasts and pressed them in so that sometimes her breath caught and sparks flew in front of her eyes. She sat by a clump of stones, closed her eyes and pictured her bedroom where she could see herself lying on her bed, untying her swimsuit, peeling it down to her waist, sensing her sweat dry away and the heat of the room not quite warm enough to prevent her shiver.

'Excuse me', said a male voice.

Susanne opened her eyes and saw that a long, delicate foot had spread its toes on the stone above her shoulder, while its companion foot hung in the air. Water dripped from the body to which they were connected. Susanne shielded her eyes and smiled upwards, then looked back down at that pale foot. It had a large vein running from the ankle to the second toe. The toenails were pristine with white tips. She watched the foot flush pink just above its sole as it gripped the rock, while the other foot landed onto a sandy patch between stones.

'Do you mind?' said the owner.

He had silky hair cut long over his ears and Susanne had no doubt that if he pinned his hair back behind them, he'd look female.

'I'm Jon', he said and put out his hand.

She took it. 'Susanne'.

Jon nodded in the direction of the sunbathers and sea swimmers.

'Always a surprise, isn't it? The sun in an Irish summer. Maybe I notice it more because I'm not Irish'.

'What are you then?' Susanne asked.

Jon took off his sunglasses and smiled at her. She could smell coffee on his breath. His teeth were perfect.

'Canadian', he said.

'Oh well, I'm Irish'.

'I'm looking for an Irish wife', Jon said.

Susanne smiled at him. 'Sure you are'.

'I'm very specific in what I want', he insisted.

Susanne nodded at the sea. 'You should go in there and cool off'.

'Susanne isn't a very Irish name', Jon said. His shoulder glanced off hers as he turned to study her. 'You look very Irish, though ... fair hair, fair skin'.

Susanne returned his stare. 'Okay ... what do you look like then?'

'My mother was half-Chinese', Jon said. 'My father was a small Dutchman from outside Amsterdam'. He breathed in and his rib bones stuck out.

Jesus, Susanne thought. Am I about to be picked up by a thin, useless tourist?

But then she looked at Jon's feet. They were milk coloured with blue veins, while her feet had a robust yellow hue with dry flaking heels. Susanne crabbed her toes into the sand to hide her dirty nails.

'I'm hardly interested in being a wife', she announced.

Jon shrugged. 'No problem, Susanne. If it's not you, then it's someone else'.

Susanne said, 'Why Irish?'

'Romance', he said.

'Oh, for God's sake, that's only made up'.

'You look like an Irish colleen'.

'I look like shit and you could be a serial killer or a stalker'.

Jon studied Susanne's straight shoulders and her swimsuit-flattened breasts, her legs, then her knees and her feet.

'You should protect your skin', he said. 'You'll burn'.

'I like getting hot', she replied.

Susanne shut her eyes against the beach glare and wished this Jon would vanish. Jesus ... an Irish wife ... every summer brought the idiot romantics, but usually she ignored them. She gazed across the bodies in the sea, over heads, arms and kids in plastic rings until she saw her two friends waving at her. Susanne waved back. Her friends used sign language to tell her something, but Susanne wasn't interested.

She heard Jon shift and noticed his shadow crawl and dip between the rocks. She could smell his fresh sweat. She closed her eyes and her ears picked up his breathing and the garbled noises of the beach. She concentrated on her tight swimsuit and the pleasure it forced on her breasts and she moved her head in the direction of Jon's smell. She flexed her right foot and felt his left one slip beside hers.

It made her jerk and nearly made her come. The smooth, lukewarm skin of his foot across hers; the bridge of her foot locking into the arch of his, and then his lips just under her chin, then his teeth nipping a line to her collar bone.

Sand scratched between their legs. The weight of his foot dug hers deeper into the sand. She thought of her bedroom, the window open on hot days, the sunlight marking out the shadows of wardrobe, bed and desk; her sweat drying because of the tinge of cold that was always present. She shivered and he felt it.

She opened her eyes. His head was below her collarbone, his mouth above her breasts. She touched the base of his neck. She took only shallow breaths, all the more to feel a drag of pleasure. If he bit, then it would be perfect.

'Susanne?'

Susanne looked up after a few seconds. Her two friends stood dripping seawater and they hung onto their towels for something to hold while their mouths remained open.

'Susanne?' they said.

Susanne didn't bother answering, but closed her eyes, willing Jon to bite, which he did, which meant she married him that autumn.

The Only Man in the World

Bernard swallowed hot water with lemon and it cut through his gut. Then he shaved with slow strokes, easing over his Adam's apple while he sang just a little. It was too early to think, so he just let his mind wander thick and grey over the insides of the quiet house. Sometimes he could almost believe that June was dead after all. The house held no sound of her; not even of her sleeping. There was only the plop of shaving foam into the sink water, his humming and the soft buzz of morning outside the mosquito-netted window.

Bernard ran his thumb over the razor blade and a narrow cut of blood seeped out. He shivered inside, breathed deep enough to see his nostrils move in his reflection. His chest was pasty white still, but from the top of his biceps down his freckles had darkened and joined up. They gave him a schizophrenic tan, dark brown in places, beige-white and dirty cream.

The blood from his thumb trickled to a dry point just above his elbow. He cleared his throat, then listened. June did not stir. Sometimes he wondered what would happen if she did die in her sleep. He wondered how long it would take for him to notice.

June hadn't said anything for three days and Bernard knew he could not last for much longer. Her silence turned her into a robot. It made her face grey and her lips thin. Bernard hated kissing her when she was like that.

Women were supposed to kiss you and they were supposed to mew with delight when they kissed you. They were not supposed to shake or freeze into silence. June did not do things right. Bernard remembered how good she used to be, but that was before the marriage; and in Rome, Bernard had realised that he didn't like the way she was more interested in statues and paintings or how she got lost in filthy little shops to finger postcards of sad women drawn by useless artists. They were all dead and gone now, yet they had still trapped his wife and made her face come more alive than he ever could.

Bernard walked back into the bedroom and took his watch from the bedside table. He sat on the edge of the bed and waited for June to say something. He could hear her breathing in a slow regular pattern. He could not tell if she was faking it or not. He turned to look at her. Her belly disgusted him a little. It was as if she held it like a weapon against him. That brown narrow line from her belly button to her crotch made him think that any moment now and the thing inside would unzip the line, put its two little hands on either side and go 'Peek a boo Daddy!'

Bernard hadn't meant to kick her there. That's what he told her. That's what he believed. He knew that was what he believed.

It was just that she did things that she knew she shouldn't. She moved too slow around the kitchen and she was too small for the bulbous belly.

'I want to come into town with you', June had said.

'It isn't a real town', he had said back. 'I told you that before'.

'It's got a post office, Bernard. It's got shops'.

'You are not coming', he said.

She gave him the same look as she had given him in Rome and in the long seconds before he hit her, there was a boiling pulse of joy from his gut to his fist, then the shock as the blow went through her face and the way she fell soft – like a cloth doll – to her knees.

He had stood over her breathing hard. He could not stop smiling. He kicked her. June didn't scream, but she moaned deep from where the baby came from and bunched her green cotton dress in her fists.

That was three days ago and June had not said a word since.

Bernard put on his clothes. He whistled some tune he had heard from the radio. In the beginning they used to dance to music, or she did, sweeping her arms and turning on her heels while he watched her. He watched her pretty face, the twist of her hips and feet and the long curve from her wrists to her shoulders. He'd watch her talk to people with that open smile of hers and giggle like a little girl. He wanted that. He wanted her and when she was pregnant, things just got planned.

'I'm sorry', Bernard said into the darkness.

June's breathing changed pitch and pace and that gave Bernard hope. He knew things would be better when he returned. Everything followed a pattern. It was like his routine of shaving. You start off messy then you clean up.

'I'm sorry, June'.

It was important to say it a second time. He fixed his collar and closed his eyes and somehow the tears came. He squeezed them through and his voice thickened with phlegm. He knew she would have noticed.

'I'll bring you back something', he said.

June said nothing but her head moved.

Bernard reached for his keys. June shifted in the bed, opened her eyes and stared at the ceiling. Bernard didn't look at her. He stood in the middle of the room and managed to look as if he was thinking of something else other than her belly and the green bruises on her face.

But he had to say it, he had to show some little fear and it slipped out like broken glass in his words. He presumed this is what you said when things got quieter. You had to show something; you had to try to feel something.

'You will put make-up on, won't you ... in case someone visits?'

He walked out of the room and found his briefcase. He unlocked the front door and stepped out onto the veranda. The morning heat wrapped him tight. He could feel sweat in his groin and under his arms. He puffed his cheeks and looked at the sharp horizon. The sun was sliding upwards. He wanted to be right at its centre. Use it as a vector point and follow a trajectory down from the lip of Nigeria into the arm pit of the Cameroon then onwards to the Congo where his French would be useful.

When he was a child he used to pin-point the atlas. He never meant to start off in Nigeria. He never meant to be what he was now – teaching French in a bush school too far off from the road to Benin and married for some other reason besides love. He had wanted to walk in Marco Polo's footsteps with the colours of Venice behind him and the rolling, brilliant seas ahead.

Bernard stood on the veranda step.

June opened the door behind him. Her face was dry but puffy and she was wearing an old dressing-gown.

'Bring back orange juice', she said.

He smiled and she moved against the doorway.

Bernard thought that her face looked almost pretty and once the baby was out then maybe she would go back to what she was before.

He turned and saluted the sun. 'Bonjour Monsieur Soleil'.

Sometimes Bernard felt like the only man in the world.

Corn-Swallowed Woman

I had to identify my mother's body. Your father can't do it, they told me. He's holed himself up in the old house, refuses to see anyone. But he does eat the food Mrs Carson cooks for him. She said it was the least she could do. She said it was the Christian thing to do.

The story was that some kid had been out fishing in the river beyond Dad's old cornfield. The kid had been trespassing, but that was forgotten because he got all traumatised since he found what he found. He had caught his foot on a tree root and fell into the water. The kid hauled himself back onto the river bank, bashed his rod against the root and the root snapped into tiny fingers. The boy followed the root right up along until he found the skull.

The body was identified as Julie Anderson, the woman that was swallowed up by the corn twenty odd years ago.

So I came back home and brought my wife Greta with me. She took one look at the house and the festering old man still inside it and she decided to return to the hotel in Bathurst.

'I'll pick you up in the morning', she promised.

I gazed out at what was left of Dad's corn. It had rotted from edge to edge as if the old bastard had taken a monster mower to mash it down.

Maybe he had wanted to keep Mum inside it. I pulled back from thinking about Mum. I smiled at Greta instead. She didn't smile back. She had put her sunglasses on and I focussed right on their dark centre. Greta's mouth flinched. Greta didn't really look like Mum except as an outline. Sometimes when we were in bed, I could see the angles of Mum's body, either stretched out or folded up. Greta said I had a weird way of loving her these days.

'It's like an alligator forgot its desert', the forensic pathologist had said.

But I recognised the bits and pieces left of Mum. I recognised her cheap green glass bead necklace and the threads of her dress caught along her pelvis. They had also found her old suitcase as well, buried beside her.

'A rotten death', the pathologist said. He pointed at her skull. 'Bashed in there, maybe not much blood to begin with ...' He looked at me again, then inched his gaze behind me to the waiting room beyond. 'You want ... your wife in here with you?'

But Greta hadn't wanted to see Mum. Greta was bored.

I had twelve years on Greta. I had that lived in look men get when they steer closer to forty and Greta had liked it fine for a while. She said she had that father-figure love syndrome built into her and she admired my suits and haircut. She liked the way I used to run. She liked my stories about the Greeks and she had liked my body.

'It's the way you keep your muscles in place', she said.

'Oh yeah?' I said.

'Oh yeah', she said back.

'Tell me about the Minotaur again', she used to say. Or 'Why was Ariadne such a useless dag?'

Greta also liked the boiled-up shit that was still inside me. It meant she had to dig deep for gold, and she liked to hold my face in her hands just to imagine what I'd look like if I had a real chin.

'It's as if it was God's third attempt before he got to Adam', she used to joke.

But when I began to sweat the bed with dreams of my mother, and when Mum's body was finally dug up by some eleven-year-old kid, Greta said maybe that boiled-up shit of mine was something she couldn't handle anymore.

She stood on the veranda and held out the bell of her dress to catch the late-afternoon air. I sat on the top step, smoking. I watched the cornfield from the corner of my right eye. The river had churned up. I used to fish in it as a kid. Mum used to climb one of the trees in her bare feet, hair down her back, arms wide for balance and laughing a little ... sometimes a lot.

'Mum used to wind me up', I remembered out loud. I switched my gaze to Greta. 'She used to dig her fingers into the back of my head and make me run as fast as I could'.

Greta was flicking the car keys through her fingers.

I mimed winding up the back of my neck and added special effects by cranking up a growl.

'She said she loved me so much that she was afraid of losing me'.

'You made that up', Greta said. She shoved her sun-hat back from her forehead.

'You've new freckles', I said.

'Thanks', she said.

She ran her foot over the edge of the veranda. I watched her face.

Mum had hated the sun. Dad said that was one of the reasons he married her. She had that old world aura about her, then he got her pregnant and then she stayed. He said it was love. She never said what it was, but she said I was the best thing she had made.

'She always wanted you', Dad said.

Dad was sitting at the table in the kitchen. There was a dish of cold stew in front of him and flies buzzed on the meat bones. Dad had a beer on the table and a jug of milk draped in a net doily. The radio was tuned in low to local country music.

'Where's your wife?' Dad said.

'Gone back to the hotel ... she doesn't like it out here'.

Dad spat at the feeding flies. 'You're looking old', he said.

I sat down and relaxed the chair back to balance on its hind legs.

'How's Mrs Carson's stew?'

'You know Mrs Carson', Dad said.

'Yeah?' I encouraged.

'She wears silk knickers', Dad said. He twisted his hand palm up as if he was twisting something into his old ute engine. 'All different colours to go with the days'. He wiped up spit from his lips then reached for his beer. 'I've seen it all when she fixes the curtains'.

'Good old Mrs Carson', I said.

I got up from the chair, took a warm beer from the fridge, then leaned against the old kitchen shelves where Mum used to stack her books before Dad burned them all. Greek and Roman myths with pictures of Pluto and Persephone, Clytie and Helios, Hero and Leander; old romance books and an Atlas, as well as foreign cooking recipes pasted into notebooks with pictures of me, and Dad burned them as well. He said some things you don't hang onto. Some things you don't remember, because they can rot you inside out.

Dad tucked the doily in underneath the jug of milk. The jug wobbled, then stilled. Old age had shaved him down. His white hair was patched on his skull and the blue veins bunched over his ears.

'Those bones', he said. 'How do they know it's her?'

I shifted to lean against the fridge. 'Her necklace, bits of dress', I listed for Dad on my fingers. 'Her teeth'.

We looked at each other as I finished my beer and started in on another one.

'Sometimes I see her', he said.

I kept on drinking my beer.

'Twenty years and nothing', Dad said. 'Then some kid goes fishing on my land and your mother turns up'.

Dad twisted his jaw from side to side, but kept his eyes on me.

'Saw what you did to the cornfield', I said to make his eyes move off me.

Dad cricked his neck to look out the kitchen window. 'Got tired', he said.

I turned and manoeuvred the fridge forward to examine its back. 'Your fridge is fucked, Dad'.

'Mrs Carson's still got her theories', Dad said'. She says a boy like you was too close to his mother'.

'Christ, Dad', I said.

The old man shrugged. 'You ran out of that cornfield like you were running out of hell'. He wiped his hand across his face. He sat forward in his chair as a couple of blood-boozed flies cruised up from his plate.

'Running out of hell', he said.

I looked out through the window at the melting sun. Mum had loved evenings. She said she felt she could run into them and disappear forever.

Mum and I in the kitchen and she's baking lemon cake, my favourite. She's singing and shuffling her feet in time to the radio music. She winks at me. I wink back. She reaches over and screws her flour fingers into the back of my head.

'There ... all wound up now', she says.

Mum had put on new shoes after she had baked the lemon cake. The shoes were made of green leather. Mum had let me put my hand into one of them and she snapped the clasp over my wrist.

'Like you got hooves', she had laughed.

She put on lipstick too. The cake's smell filled up the kitchen. She danced around the kitchen, while she filled up her handbag with little bits. I followed her into her and Dad's room. She picked up a picture of me and put it in her bag. She got some perfume, then she put on her jacket and took up her suitcase, opened the front door and the sun was halfway down the sky.

Dad reached over and picked off a fly from the congealed meat grease. He held the insect up. Its wings buzzed just above his fingernails. Its legs were rigid – stuck in fat.

'I knew she had someone', Dad said, as if he were explaining the whole thing to someone else. 'I could smell it off her'.

Dad dropped the fly onto his plate. Its wings buzzed twice, before he pressed his thumb down and killed it.

After Mum disappeared, Dad used to sit there late at night waiting for her to come back somehow. Later, he brought women back from Bathurst and beyond. They'd look at him, then at me, and one or two might have wondered how they could fit in here, but they never stayed long enough to find out.

Then I started running. Running so fast it was like I was flying.

'You should have married again', I told him.

Dad got up from the table and dumped the meat leftovers into the plastic bag that hung from the door underneath the kitchen sink. I left him there and I was halfway down the hall when he called after me.

'I use it for my tools mostly, but your bed is still in there'.

My old window was nailed shut. Mum had painted butterflies on the glass, but they were long gone now. 'I should never have married your father', she used to tell me whenever she got drink-dreamy.

'Should have married somebody like you', Mum said.

You read the Greek myths and there it is, all that mother love just waiting to drown you and when it happens you think, Mum's young ... she looks like a girl sometimes and she likes dancing and when she's in bed with you, your guts boil over inside because she tells stories about boys like you, boys just like you, that she should have loved instead of that man in the other room.

Dad followed me down.

'Anything you left behind is in a box somewhere', he said as he shifted about the room. His breathing filled up the room. I rang Greta's mobile, but she didn't answer.

'Sit down, Dad. Give your lungs a rest'.

Dad shoved the old curtains off a chair and sat down. The silence between us heightened the heat in the room, but I pushed through it the same way I had pushed through the cornfield, the same way I'd push through a race.

The thing with running is you shut out the world. You get as close to God, or to somewhere else, the darkness, the light, the goddamn anywhere you can escape into, and you keep on running until you are too tired to exist anymore.

Mum used to say it was the small things that murdered you in the end. Greta used to say she loved me because I wouldn't let her in as far as she wanted to go. She wanted to dig her hands deep into my shit and smooth it into nothing. You want it so much you can taste it, and then you don't want it anymore.

Dad took a cigarette from his shirt pocket.

I wanted to turn the light off and stretch out. I knew Mum wouldn't come back, but I wanted to feel as if she might just come in the door and creep up to sit beside me and tell me a story first of all. Just a story that she had read in one of those library books of hers. She told me once that good stories led onto the proper endings.

'I did save you, didn't I, son?'

'Yeah, Dad', I said.

I closed my eyes and I could feel Mum next to me, fitting in where Greta never could, where no one ever could. Almost the same way she had fitted into the river bank where Dad had buried her.

I opened my eyes. I didn't want to see that ending. I didn't want to see the rock and the blood and Dad's eyes or his hands as he fixed her into the hole. He had said the river bank was thousands of years old, but the edges would never fall in. I didn't want to remember that Dad killed Mum and that Mum just had this smile on her face because she couldn't believe she was being killed.

Instead I just saw myself running back through the cornfield, back to where Dad should have been all the time, fixing his old ute, squeezing his eyes up at the sun then across at the breeze-blown yellow-living cornfield like it hid nothing inside.

I ran back so fast, I felt I was flying.

And all the time I was flying, I was re-winding.

The Extraordinaire

On a hot morning in July nineteen-twenty-one, Alice and Martin arrived in Brighton. They sat watching the sea, while others watched them.

People noticed Alice and Martin. She, for her beauty which she had always been used to, her turquoise eyes and remarkable face, pale and elongated, a living Modigliani with her chin-length dark hair and dark pink mouth, and he, for his quivering head which Alice took care to ignore as best she could. She nibbled some chocolate and thought again what she meant to do. It would be managed, she decided.

Martin did not move beside her. He had hardly spoken to her, except once to remind her that the whole thing wasn't particularly necessary. He was no longer her lover, he was someone else's. He had such pride in him, as he told her. He was Thomas's now. Thomas let him breathe. Thomas demanded nothing.

But Martin was still beautiful to Alice. She had never forgotten that. In the beginning his flinching head and animal eyes had been a challenge to her, one that had galvanised her idea of loving him.

'Thomas was right', Alice said out loud. 'A day away. Just perfect'.

She looked at Martin's face, at his scars, not all from the war, but from his own hand, and also from hers. They only heightened his beauty for her. She remembered the night he had demanded she slit his throat and, in fear, in fascination, she had held the knife at his jugular, his pleading, furious eyes on her, his breath on her sweating fingers, and she had wondered then if he did die, how would it be afterwards? How would she be without him?

Yet life would return to normal, as it always did whenever anyone left Alice. Thomas described it as her only ordinary flaw.

'You will people away', he said.

'Do I?' she wondered sometimes. But she rarely wished to understand – life was good despite the times alone, and usually another lover would slot in, filling those odd moments when she must have someone else; moments she could not describe aloud to anyone, but they were like blades in her gut.

Martin had regularly begged to die. He crawled beneath their bed to be away from her and she often left him there, returning later to find him at the kitchen table trying to write any story that came into his head. Sometimes he read it out to her and made her jealous. His words got into people. They got into her. People saw in their minds what he wrote on the page.

I should have loved him more, thought Alice.

Thomas had been cruel when he agreed to her plan for the day. He had laughed to begin with while he fixed his tie and then rubbed his teeth clean with one finger. He put on a show, demanding a shave from his new butler, moving about his *boudoir* where she had often been. The light caught on his collection of glass and gold figurines, and he wondered aloud why she would request such a thing.

She shrugged and said she wanted to say goodbye. She said she deserved that much.

'I loved him once', she said.

'You were curious once', Thomas told her.

Alice had known Thomas ever since she had arrived in London. He helped her change her accent, so that it contained just the underlay of an Irish brogue. It kept her exotic, but approachable. He stood her in front of a mirror and ordered her to adopt Grecian poses. She had the correct lines, like a milk-coloured, untouchable boy and only her long hair and unlikely beautiful face – more beautiful without expression – meant she was a woman.

Thomas taught Alice that the necessities of life depended on how much people wanted to be used by others.

And Alice developed her natural ability to use. She put it down to curiosity. Those who suffered fascinated her. She appreciated suffering. She liked to imagine the horror involved with such pain and how it could be so powerful as to leave its mark. She felt such a difference needed patronage and Alice became known for her odd choices. Even prostitutes from the street caught her eye. Thomas maintained it was 'dabbling', living life second-hand in order to spice up her published stories.

She had tried other methods. She began stories in her own fashion, stories she thought she might remember from her home and childhood. Her grandfather had owned two horses that he had loved. Her mother loathed smelling of the farm and rarely ate. There had been brothers and sisters, but Alice had forgotten them. Too Irish to remember. Too noisy. Too dirty.

Her father had loved Mass and admired the local priest's notions, one of which was that Alice had an intelligent face and should continue with her education.

Alice continued. It meant her way out. She was sent to Dublin and lost her virginity after a night out at a local cheap opera. She adored clothes that said she was somebody. Clothes of deep colours – purple, blues, crimson, black jet beads and silk underwear.

Yet all this education never fit into what she wrote. It had no flow, Thomas informed her. So Alice wrote stories of the people that she found, and most of them accepted her plunder since she paid well.

She became known. She was 'The Extraordinaire', capable of discovering people who became talking points in conversations, people who usually had a unique talent, and then drifted off into being part of the crowd and sometimes discovered their own niche. Others were more strange and soon disappeared, but all of them found their way into her stories.

Alice smiled out to the sea. A hot, busy day in Brighton had never been part of her imagined ending. In the beginning, she and Martin had done everything together. They had holidayed with exciting friends and lived life on a comfortable edge. They spent a summer in Paris, without Thomas, and there for a brief six weeks Alice made love to a sculptor, while Martin attended an analyst. That had failed when Alice discovered him staring into the mirror, his knuckles dug into his head and his whole body carved with that intense, dangerous effort that she had lusted after, now directed only at his reflection.

'You're forgetting me', she accused him.

Brighton promenade wearied Alice. It was too crowded, too full of band music and children licking ices. She touched Martin's hand. It didn't move beneath her fingers.

When Alice had first seen Martin, she had wanted him. He was a late arrival to Thomas's party and he found a seat next to a naked well-breasted woman who hummed to music. She was popular with everyone. She dangled her legs across Martin's lap and laughed at anyone's funny story. Alice didn't need to know her name. Girls like that had nothing in them, and if they had, it was buried deep under drugs and wine. A girl like that would only fill out two sentences in a story.

But Martin was different. It was nineteen-nineteen and he was a sudden and promising writer. He had suffered in the war and his face had deep lines on each side of his mouth. His red-blonde hair was thick and shone as he bent every so often to kiss the girl's breasts.

Thomas laid his fingers on Alice's shoulder.

'They make a startling picture', he approved. 'A shivering head and laughing breasts'.

'He might hear you, Thomas'.

'He's piss-poor and dirty. Like him, Alice?'

'Interesting', replied Alice.

'He loves being interesting', Thomas said. 'All new writers do. It's like a currency with them. Better than food. Certainly an improvement on sex'.

Thomas kissed Alice's cheek. 'My beautiful half-boy', he said.

Alice felt his smooth skin and inhaled hard on her cigarette. He kissed her beneath her long earrings.

'Beware your curiosity, Alice'.

Alice ignored his smile and shook away from his grasp. Thomas gave a low bow, fixed his hand on some pretty thing and was drawn off. Alice turned to see Martin watching her. He flipped the naked girl's legs from his lap, stood and also bowed.

'Alice Roe', he said. 'The Extraordinaire'.

They danced together.

'I've read your work', she lied.

He gave a wide and desperate smile and Alice saw that he was missing two back teeth.

'And?' he demanded.

Alice admired his approach. Most new writers insisted on being coy.

'I like it all', she said.

He nodded. His lips were thin. A little spittle had collected at one corner of his mouth. A side effect of his head shaking, she assumed. She pressed close against him.

'I always wanted to write', he said. 'Always'.

Alice smiled. 'It's obvious', she remarked.

His gaze juddered away from her, across the room and the faces watching him dance with her.

'You're famous, Alice'.

'Thank you', she said.

He kissed her neck. She laughed and held her fingers beneath his chin. His head shook harder.

'Nothing stops it', he warned her.

She asked him about his home and he replied that he had none. A mother dead three years and a father still drunk in a Suffolk village. Later, in his iron bed with her back against the damp, papered wall, Alice read his work.

He wrote that he no longer loved God. He wrote about the dirt men grasped as they died. He wrote his soul down on paper and Alice finally said:

'I think we all want to forget about the war'.

His shoulders were bony and pale against hers. She kissed his forehead and said:

'Write about happier things'.

Martin's kisses trembled on her face and his fingers liked to hurt, but Alice developed a tolerance for all of that. At night he whispered his nightmares into her throat. His sweat made her smell and she had to have sponge baths everyday. He wrote as she advised, but even then his soul crept into his stories, displaying a savage pain she did not want to see. The pain she had seen in the prostitutes, in odd and various lovers, in her own forgotten parents, all of whose pain she had once filtered into her work, now lived in Martin's.

'A writer', declared Thomas.

Thomas had christened the whole episode: 'Alice's Heathcliff Holiday'. He arranged parties in which Martin took centre stage as well as Thomas's attention.

'You'll use him', Alice accused.

'He'll survive it', Thomas replied.

Alice saw Thomas's smooth skin against Martin's patched face. Her insides cracked as she understood now that she was losing something she had hardly ever known. By the kitchen table, she read Martin's stories and realised how she had failed. She had nothing of his brilliance. She pressed her hand against her heart, then ripped at her clothes until she felt it beat.

It was normal and there was still something she could not understand, an ... emptiness, and only Martin's stories reached inside.

And now finally as they walked along the pier, Alice decided to say something absolute and brave; something she could write into a story. Something no one could ever expect of her.

'Tell me to leave', she told Martin. 'Tell me to leave so that I can'.

She stared into his shattered face. She tried to follow his gaze, tried to will his eyes to fill her, but it was useless.

He said goodbye first and left her there. She lingered for a time before finding a café, then sat sideways to a half-mirrored wall. She ordered chocolate ice-cream and ate steadily. Then she looked at her reflection. She lifted her chin to see more of herself. She imagined her heart and wondered if it was as ruined as it could possibly be. Its emptiness gnawed her. There was nothing to fill it now.

Perhaps it is a broken heart, she wondered.

And she smiled at her reflection and decided that suited her.

RUNT

The knife's handle stuck out from her pocket and tipped her hip as she walked across the grey, old mud. Her father walked ahead of her. He was breathing hard and his braces hung from his trousers. The ground spit up as he walked upon it. Each foot left an oozing mark, trails of mud slime on the soles of his boots.

There was a smell of pig shit. The girl ran her tongue along the inside of her mouth just to taste the remains of the chicken soup her mother had given her for breakfast. She held her breath for seconds, then blew out hard. Her breath condensed white in front of her. She focused on the mist, longing to be somewhere else.

She did not like killing pigs. She did not like looking into their eyes and fearing that they were a little bit human inside. Pigs were intelligent. Pigs had human eyes, her father once told her, and the Devil's feet. That's why we kill them. That's why we eat them.

The girl had never believed that story, but every time she dug the knife into a pig's throat, its blood boiled upwards and smelled like hot iron.

To kill a pig was not unlike killing a man, her father had also told her. You take the throat in almost the same way. The daughter tried hard not to look at her father's hands when he spoke like that. They were crossed with lines and dirt from the vegetables, dirt from the pigs. He had often tried to clean them, to make them as perfect as they could be.

He used gun oil sometimes. He'd sit in the shed on an upturned bucket with a bowl of oil into which he'd dip his fingers, then slather up as far as his wrists and sing a song he had learned from the militia.

His daughter knew by now that the gun oil cleaned nothing, but it was useful to shift the ingrained dirt. She watched globs of scum collect in her father's palms, which he flicked at his daughter who squealed, sidestepped and deliberately kept laughing because she had seen what her father's hands could do.

'Your father is a brave man', the girl's boyfriend said as they drank cheap beer in his new car.

The girl said yes.

Her boyfriend smelled so good. He liked being clean. He also liked his girlfriend's blonde hair, and, although she wore the clothes he brought back to her, she liked books too much.

He once went into her bedroom with her father's permission and found where she hid the books. She had cut a hole in the wall so well that the seam was hidden in the wood grain. She must have learned that from her father.

She was angry, but scared. Her father had piled the books one on top of the other on the kitchen table. She did not look at him. Not until he told her to. And when she did, she remembered how she had once seen people on their knees – boys and men mostly – ready to fall back into their graves, yet some had lifted their faces and looked at their killers.

'They are all pigs', her father had preached. 'You kill pigs before they kill you'.

The little boys didn't look up. They clung to their fathers. They wet themselves, cried for their mothers who had been raped, burned to death or were still alive somewhere else. Little boys in their school uniforms or pyjamas dug their fingers into the arms of men who knelt beside them. The little boys wanted to go home. Once or twice they looked up into the watching crowd and saw a school friend, but the friend was told to spit on them.

Some of the men would pretend to be a boy's father – if the father was already dead – and would hold the boy in his arms to hide him from his own death. But one boy would not stop crying for his mother. A gun was put in his mouth and fired. The man holding the boy screamed as if his heart was being ripped out.

The girl looked at her mother who sat in a chair and stared at the books.

'This is what you spend your money on?'

'They are just books', the daughter replied.

'Burn them', her mother ordered.

The girl burned the books one by one.

She had developed into a good pig killer and by now she could kill by touch. She had learned not to look at the pig's eyes, but to straddle its neck, while her father held its haunches down. She had strong arms and hooked her left elbow about the animal's neck. She swallowed down the feeling in her own throat as she held her knife in her other hand. Her father had made it to fit her palm, blade at her fingertips. You feel for the pulse, then you plunge the knife in straight.

You release the pig. It stumbles. It looks at you and you think how human the look is. It moves forward and its blood gushes. You don't want to cry, but you want to do something. Your own body is empty. You want to faint and not wake up.

She had once asked her father: 'When did you stop?'

Her father had slung the pig onto a hook to drain the blood. Outside the other pigs were restless, and a sow was feeding. The girl's father had stopped to check them before he had suspended the dead pig. He pointed out a runt, clicked his teeth and winked at his daughter.

'When did you stop?' she asked him.

He glanced at her. 'Stop what?'

'Killing people', she said.

Her father laughed. 'What people?' Her father kept on laughing and slapped the pig. It swayed on its hook. 'That was war', he told his daughter. 'It was war and we had a right'.

'I don't like killing pigs', his daughter said. 'I don't like the smell and I don't like eating them'.

'We eat pigs', her father said. 'We don't have cows'.

'I don't want to kill another pig', the girl said.

Her father took her outside to the sow that was feeding its litter. He scooped up the runt and then placed its wriggling body under his boot. He crushed down. The runt's skull burst outwards. The girl's father picked up the runt's body by its tail and flung it at his daughter's feet.

'Give it to the dog'.

The girl buried the runt instead and she thought if she said a prayer then the sound of its baby skull splitting would leave her head, but it didn't. Nothing seemed safe or right until the moment she told her boyfriend that she wanted to leave.

'And go where?'

'Where you go', she said.

Her boyfriend liked to drink and smoke in the back room of his friend's house. His friend was listening to music with earphones strapped to his head. His friend's mother was polishing her jewellery. She smiled at the girl and the girl whispered into her boyfriend's ear.

'And I don't want to come back'.

Her boyfriend calculated something in his head. He looked at the girl's face, at her skin and noticed how rough her hands were.

'You will have to make them soft', he said. 'They don't like hands like that in the West'. He kissed her knuckles. 'I'll give you something. It can be a present'.

The girl gave some of the hand cream to her mother and grandmother. They laughed as their fingers slipped in and out of each other's.

Her boyfriend had told the girl to use it all over her body and each time she moved in her bed, the smell of her skin made her feel beautiful – no longer a pig killer.

When they reached Berlin, the girl finally persuaded her boyfriend to buy her some perfume. He hadn't liked spending the money, but she told him that she would pay him back when she got a hairdressing job.

'Maybe you would like another job', he said.

'No', she said.

His friend had laughed and said what a waste. The girl didn't understand his laugh. They were sitting in the back of another friend's car. She was in the middle. The friend put his hand on her knee. She jerked away, then laughed, because she was surprised. His hand lifted for a few seconds, then landed on her thigh, high above her knee.

Her boyfriend was looking out of the car window. The driver glanced in the rear-view-mirror. The friend was singing, tapping along the girl's thigh and in time to the song on the car radio. The girl dug her elbow into her boyfriend's ribs. He turned and smiled at her, shrugged, then resumed staring out of his window.

The girl shoved the friend's hand away. His own surprise was nearly funny and she wanted to laugh, to make things good again, but he hit her on the upper part of her face. The force snapped her head back and the last thing she remembered was how the red-ribbed roof of the car looked like the inside of a mouth.

An Incident in the Bedroom

Never could remember when I started hating my younger sister, but it had been in me a long time. It wasn't even the day when she sashayed up to me and said, 'You know the village boys screw their sisters?'

I choked on my beer and almost fell of the veranda. My friend David nearly pissed himself laughing.

'Fuck', he crowed. 'Fuck your sister, man'.

I punched him and his beer spun into the air as he crumpled to his knees. I grabbed his head and yelled into his face what kind of sick bastard says that kind of shit?

'Jesus ... Jesus ... Theo', David said, and held his hands up. 'It's a joke. It's only fun'.

I dropped him and turned to look at Marianne, who shrugged and said, 'It's the truth'.

'Screw you, Marianne'.

'Theo, man, your sister knows what's what'.

'Yeah, Theo. I know what's what'.

I hated the way Marianne stood as if she were far older than seventeen. She stood like a mini-whore in shorts with one leg standing sideways, so David could see her whole inner thigh.

'Wear some clothes', I said.

'Make me'.

I leaned back against the veranda pillar with another beer from the cooler bag and said:

'Get lost, little girl. Big boys want to talk'.

I burped and David burped back. Marianne was disgusted and flounced off. David reached for another beer, but I grabbed it first. He looked at me.

'Sorry', I said and handed the beer over.

'No problem, Theo'.

'Shit my sister says pisses me off', I explained.

'Yeah', David said. He peeled back, drank, then said, 'But she's right, you know. All those weasels fuck their sisters. It's bred into them. Ever look at their kids? Eyes in the wrong places and shit ... all fucking deformed. Hitler had the right idea about shit like that. Just get rid of what you don't need. Clean the place up'.

'Sure', I said.

'Yeah, you know what I'm talking about. They aren't like us. They'll never be us. That guy they executed last week ...? Had his picture taken with the Commies from overseas ...?'

'Yeah, what about him?'

David gargled then gulped more beer. 'Fucked his sister', he said.

'Bullshit', I said.

David shrugged. 'It's documented. Signed the admission just before they hung the prick'.

'Sure?'

'I saw it'.

'The hanging or the admission?'

'He couldn't even write', David continued. 'Scribbled some mark. I'm going to get a copy and hang it up ... look cool on my wall'.

'Did you watch the hanging, David?

David was looking over my shoulder. Staring at nothing. I looked as well. Just the jasmine tree standing full with white flowers and some kids playing ball down by the swings ...

David shivered, then grinned. 'Just making sure', he said. He slapped my back, then wiped his face. He wasn't sweating, but he was jumping. His lips rubbed against each other.

'You eating sherbet?' I said, using our old word for it.

'Fucking awful mess', David said.

'Yeah?'

'They always try to stay alive'. David mimed the look. 'Piss and shit come running out'. He reached into the bag for more beer, popped the tab, paused and looked at me.

'Ever want to draw one?'

'No', I said.

'It'd be cool', David said. 'It'd be different to what you usually do'.

I said nothing and sat back up on the veranda wall. I wanted to forget where I was. I wanted the small crowd of people at the other end of the veranda to disappear. I wanted it to be night. A thick, soft night that held the whole day's sweat inside its dark gut. Those kinds of nights made me invincible. I could imagine anything those nights.

I focussed my eyes on some new plant Mum had wound round the pillar in front of me. Dark green, no flower. I could paint that, I told myself. Mum made sure things looked good. Things always had to look good.

'I like what I do', I said to David.

'Yeah, well what the fuck do I know?' David smiled. He turned and skimmed over the crowd. 'I'm the philistine who likes cars and girls, Theo. You paint pictures of pretty little flowers and I drive the girls'.

David punched my arm. 'Seriously, ever think of doing different pictures?'

David's smile was on full-force and my skin went cold. I went calm. I even raised my eyebrows and spat hard against the dark green plant on the pillar.

'No interest', I said. 'I'm a fucking botanist, or I will be when I graduate'. I nodded at the plant. 'That gets me juiced'.

David picked his fingers in between the plants stem and leaves. David had big fingers. I had seen them on Marianne.

'Watching someone die gets me juiced', he said.

He wanted my reaction but I'm like Mum. I keep everything behind my face, and the sick thing about David was that he looked like his mother when he smiled. His mother had been cool. Long and toffee-coloured tanned. I painted her many times, and at night I'd hold my penis in my hand and imagine loving her. She was sweet. I could have taken care of her. I could have said to her ... yeah all this shit gets to me too. All the fear and keeping quiet. Those fucking games we play. I could have told her that I was different and that we were two of a kind. I think she would have liked to have known there was somebody like her who knew – who just knew – that our world was dying hard and fast, despite the things that happened in the streets and in interrogation cells in the police compound at the far edge of town; despite the satellite dishes aimed at the sky beaming only bits of the world in and bits of us back; despite the secret police with their smooth smiles and smooth guns.

But I never got to say anything like that. David's mother got into her car and gassed herself. I drew it afterwards. Some old Ford with rusting chrome and her head back against the driving seat. It was important to get the proportions right.

I pulled up the floorboards in my room and put that painting with all the others: Mum and Dad at the breakfast table; Marianne on the swings when she was young; me and her at some lake, five and four respectively; Mum reading a book with the old Zebra skin on the wall behind her; Sir in class with a dead snake wrapped his neck.

Other drawings were half-done. At first I tried dead animals, then I went onto dead humans, but I never could finish those ones. I kept the perspective long on those ones. Like Mum with her Jane Austen books ... some things you don't have to see too much, if you don't look so hard.

So I put David's mother's painting right on top and at night and in bed, I'd stare at the rug that covered the exact spot, but I never managed to cry. She was still too real. I could still imagine her skin inside my arms and the sweat between her breasts. It fucked me up to look at David now.

He was still smiling. I was cool. I scanned the empty beer bag.

'I need to piss', I said. 'And we need more beer'.

I walked back through the kitchen. Joseph the cook was scraping out the insides of two rabbits.

'Hey, Joseph', I said.

Joseph looked up, then looked back down. His fingers worked fast. He rooted out the kidneys and heart. Flecks of solidified blood spattered the table-top.

'Why not use the catapult technique, Joseph?'

I grabbed an untouched rabbit and slit a knife along its belly. It was like digging a pencil in deep. I swung the rabbit up, and bent its fore and hind legs, then let fly. The rabbit's guts slapped against the opposite wall, stuck for seconds, then slid to the floor.

'Learned that in a book', I told Joseph.

Joseph had a small brown head and a thin moustache and his face was pockmarked with open pores. When I was younger I used to believe Joseph had worms in his face, with black eyes watching everything I did. I knew that's how I'd paint Joseph. I saw it in my head. I saw the fucking worms turn so their eyes could see me.

Joseph tipped some rabbit guts into a bucket. Then he took a cloth and wiped up the rabbit gut traces on the wall, and I remembered I had to piss, so I headed for the bathroom.

I liked the bathroom. It helped me think. I had ideas in this bathroom. Made my fingers itch to get the pictures down. Pictures crept into my head as if they crept into a church. I could see that if I were different, then I could walk out of my parents' house, walk down to the village, buy a drink, screw a girl if I wanted and make it home alive. Or I could imagine I was an artist who drew what he saw and hoped he'd survive.

A knock on the bathroom door and I opened it. It was Marianne with a bottle of vodka and David behind her.

'Thought we could have this in your room', she said. 'We won't be missed. They're too busy getting drunk. Dad's showing off his old guns and David's dad is crying'.

David shrugged and led us back to my bedroom. We sat on my bed and drank from the bottle. David watched Marianne's thighs, while I watched him.

'You're going to miss her', I said.

David slurped vodka. 'Who?'

'Your mother, you prick'.

'Yeah, I'll miss her'. He leaned down and smacked a kiss on Marianne's cheek. 'Just like any other mother'.

'Our mother is a neurotic', Marianne giggled.

'Shut up', I warned her.

David glanced around my room then at the paintings on my walls.

'Thought you said you were only interested in plants. I see a shit load of other things here as well. That's you, Marianne ... how old are you?'

'Eleven', I said.

'I'm telling you man ... you've a gift'.

David was right. I had a gift. His mother saw it straightaway during one of those coffee mornings Mum had organised. I was home for the weekend and I stank from a football game. Mum tried to steer me away, but David's mother had seen me. She came up close, so close I could smell her too ... came up very close, I could have touched her.

'I was in your room', she said. 'I got lost after visiting the bathroom and there was a paintbrush on the floor near your door. I got curious'.

'Theo is going to be a botanist', Mum said.

David's mother said, 'I like what Theo paints'.

She smiled over the rim of her coffee cup. Her arms were gleaming brown and she wore a dark red dress tied at her waist. She didn't look old. She looked beautiful. She looked that way when I first painted her.

'Your mother was beautiful', I said out loud.

'She was mad', David said. He screwed a finger into the side of his head. Marianne giggled again. I could hear her swallow her vodka in little baby gulps. She took a deep breath, raised her eyebrows at me, then clamped her lips over the bottle one more time.

'Watch it', I told her.

She swallowed, handed the bottle to David, then licked up any dribbles around her mouth. David leaned over and kissed her. Marianne squealed and play-slapped his face away, but she didn't fight back much when he pulled at her feet, so that her whole body faced him.

'She wasn't mad', I said.

Marianne looked back at me. 'What did you say?'

'David's mother wasn't mad and David knows it'.

'Well, she's dead now', Marianne said.

David kissed Marianne's toes. She squealed again and bounced on the bed. The vodka bottle fell sideways and spilled on my jeans. I picked it up, swallowed from it, then put it on the windowsill.

Marianne was still squealing.

'Shut up', I told her.

Marianne stuck out her tongue. I reached up for the bottle and threw it at her face. It hit her nose and blood spurted out her nostrils and into her hands.

David freaked. He screamed and scrambled off the bed. He stood in the middle of the room with Marianne's blood spray on his face. His mouth was opening and closing. I hung onto the bottle's neck. It felt really good.

There was a knock at the door and, when no one entered, I knew it was a servant.

'Come in', I said.

Joseph came in. His face didn't change when he saw the blood and the way Marianne was using my sheets to mop at her nose. Joseph moved further into the room, level with David. Marianne was still squealing like a little stuck pig.

Joseph nodded at David. 'Your father wants you'.

Maybe the blood had frightened David. Maybe it was the way Joseph relayed the message. Maybe there are lots of reasons why David did what he did. Marianne says some people go mad for seconds, but then they're alright when everything is over. Maybe it was because Joseph smiled minutely. I thought he did anyway and so did David, because he punched Joseph's face so hard that his head snapped backwards, then forwards, and there was the inevitable sound of the old man's neck cracking.

He folded down, his legs stuck out from under his torso and he sat, broken and dead in the middle of the room.

Not one of us moved.

'Is he dead?' David asked.

Marianne turned and snarled at me. 'Look at what you've done'.

'I didn't kill him', I said.

She lifted her bloody fingers in front of my face. 'I don't mean him!' She pointed at her nose. 'I mean my "dose"!'

I laughed at her. I screwed up my body and I laughed. I laughed because I was shaking. I laughed because Marianne's squealing was too loud and I had to drown it out. I laughed because Marianne couldn't see what was in front of her nose.

I heard David laughing as well. I looked up at him and he had drifted back up against the wall, but he was still staring at Joseph.

'You could draw that, couldn't you?' David said.

I stopped laughing. I looked at Joseph. His eyes were staring at me. He was sitting in almost the exact spot David's mother once sat for me. I knew what I was seeing. I was seeing a dead man in my room.

'He asked for it', David said.

Marianne pulled her feet up onto the bed. She got small and scared.

'Theo?' she said. 'Theo?'

I didn't answer her.

FAIRY TALE

Fairy tales have happy endings, but there is a point in most fairy tales where the alchemy turns sour. It happened when Snow White's father married for the second time. It happened when Sleeping Beauty pricked her finger. It happened when Rumpelstiltskin bartered a woman's future child in return for the secret of gold spun from straw.

And it also happened in this story when Eddie's wife Judith came home with a dog one evening.

The dog was a West Highland mongrel. It yapped at the birds in Eddie's aviary. It unfurled its lips and growled at Eddie. It squirmed on its back for his wife to rub its stomach. She fed it white yogurt on the kitchen linoleum. She washed its paws and picked ticks from its hair. The children loved it.

Eddie said he didn't want a dog in the house. It was like an extra kid, he said.

'Who did you buy it from?' he asked Judith. She looked good these days. She wore her hair caught up in a halo. She hadn't done that for a long time.

Judith shrugged. 'No one you'd know'. She looked in the bathroom mirror, licked her forefinger, then shaped her eyebrows while the dog sat at her feet. Some nights it slept with her in the extra bedroom.

Then Judith became pregnant for the third time and that was a surprise to Eddie.

Something flashed into his brain like a magic picture flashes into a witch's goblet. His mother dripping her hair into his face as she washed him in the bath ... Eddie could see how her stomach was pouched out. He had known what was inside; something that delighted his father, something that made his mother not his anymore.

All fairy-tales have buried secrets. Eddie's was so buried that it was like something he had read in a horror comic when he was a kid. When he thought about it, something riddled through his spine.

'I don't want another kid, Judith'.

Eddie could remember how he had loved his wife. He remembered how she smoked his cigarettes as she read him stories while he lay on her bed, watching her, watching the sunlight on her skin. Like spun gold, he had told her.

He mentioned that his mum had stopped reading him fairytales after his little brother died and Judith believed him. He also mentioned that he didn't trust big families. The way they wound themselves around each other – the way they had to love each other.

One kid for me and one for you, he had bargained with Judith.

And later when she read stories to their daughters, Eddie could still see the black vines that garrotted castle walls and the squashed up men that hid under bridges. He could see 'Roses Red' and 'Violets Blue' – young women with names that belonged on paint pots, but Judith had put them into fairy stories and made them slay dragons that had fed on abandoned babies. Those women ... those women – they loved men with that same strange kind of relish that Judith had used on Eddie and that Eddie's mother had used on Eddie's dead little brother.

In a fairy tale you have to first bury your secret deep. In a fairy tale, you bury it under a Yew tree or an Oak; or in the guts of a cave where the Devil might walk, but you don't talk about it. Then you bury it inside psychiatric sessions and gloss it up thick with all the promises of a new you, a good you and you learn to live with what you are. You learn to live with your mother's face torn open with screams. What have you done, Eddie ... what have you done? You learn to live with that invisible emptiness inside you. You go back for check-ups. You look in the mirror and you see an ordinary man. You fall in love with a woman who smiles like your mother used to smile at you. And when the babies come, you take a deep breath and you remember that you made them with Judith.

You and Judith.

This is love, Eddie told himself. This has to be love.

When his wife brought the baby home, Eddie sat on the patio outside. He watched his birds fly inside the aviary. As far as he knew birds didn't do a damn thing outside their genes. He looked at the dog. Dogs fucked any breed. The dog was lying on the patio steps. It looked at him.

'That bastard isn't mine', Eddie said to his wife.

Judith went back into the kitchen, put the baby down in its carry cot and poured some wine. She watched her husband through the French doors. For long seconds he didn't do anything, so she kept sipping her wine as she half-listened to the baby's gurgling, and right up to the second when Eddie stood with a garden chair in his hand, Judith still thought that everything was normal and complete with gurgling baby, a husband, two other kids in school and a dog sleeping on the patio steps.

Eddie beat the dog to death. It was easy to do. His wife didn't come out to save the animal. The dog barked, then screamed and Eddie had to shut out those screams. His little brother had screamed the same way and he had curled up in almost the same way ... except two legs instead of four with his arms over his head, trying to keep safe, but Eddie got him anyway.

And afterwards he had stood there staring at his brother's body, while his mother screamed and clawed at the dead mess as if she were trying to gather it back into her, bone by bone, string by string, head and all.

Eddie ... Eddie ... what have you done?

When the dog was dead, Eddie went back into the house. His wife had the baby in her arms and she was screaming. Eddie stared at the baby. Its face was screwed up in its own scream. Eddie went and got a knife from the cutlery drawer, then took an old fairy tale book from the shelf and flicked it open to a picture of Rumpelstiltskin. He gripped the knife's blade in his palm and cut into the dwarf's face.

That done, Eddie walked past his wife and into the hallway and out the front door. He sat on the front steps and watched ordinary people walk up and down the street. A few saluted him and the sun was shining so much it turned Eddie's eyesight yellow.

He didn't want to think of the dead dog or his dead brother. He didn't want to think of all the promises the doctors fed him when he was young.

You'll grow up good, Eddie, he was told.

You'll grow up good, they promised.

KILLING CALEB

Inspired by the Caleb Mayer folksong

I was knitting something small when Caleb Mayer came round with a whiskey bottle in his hand.

'Where's your husband, Nellie Cane?' he said. 'Where's your darling gone?'

I stood on the porch and looked at him. He swayed up the steps and smiled down at me.

'Where's your husband, Nellie Cane?'

I moved back just a little.

His lips shone with whiskey spittle. I held onto the porch stand and ran my toes over the bare boards.

'He's on business', I told Caleb. I looked beyond to the ridge of rocks, half-wanting to see my husband walk back over them, but he didn't come.

Caleb Meyer spat out the last of his whiskey, then dropped the bottle, grabbed my hair and threw me down on the needle bed. His elbows pressed into my belly and he grinned into my face.

'Does he know, Nellie? Does he know?' he said between his kisses.

I thought of my husband, standing sock-footed in the doorway, plucking his nails against the worm-eaten frame, saying out loud that he needed to fix it before winter, before the baby came.

I prayed God send one of your angels down. I could see the sky through Caleb's hair and his breath was filling up my mouth and he wouldn't get off me. I bit his mouth and he kept on kissing me. I kept on praying and all the time I smelled his sweat and could taste his whiskey.

Then my fingers touched the bottleneck – I broke it on the ground.

Caleb Mayer grunted. He dug one fist between my legs. My head filled cold black.

'Caleb', I said real softly and he went like a babe in my arms. I shoved his whiskey bottle just under his chin, slit one sure twist and his blood was flung out like fire.

I dragged Caleb Mayer's body all the way to the river.

'Where's your husband Nellie Cane?' he had asked me. 'Where's your darling gone?'

When he was a boy, Caleb had taught me to catch fish. He liked to hold my fingers in between his, while we waited for a fish to come into our trap.

Caleb Mayer had yellow hair then, the colour of old butter.

When he was a bit older, Caleb Mayer killed a puppy and I let him. I watched him crunch his foot onto the puppy's head and I waited for something to stop him – to make me stop him – but Caleb was laughing a laugh that got caught up in the trees and carried so high and when I looked back down the puppy's head was laid flat out with its blood and brain on the grass.

The sun was hot. It made Caleb's hair shine. He was mumbling to himself as he rubbed the puppy's blood from his toes.

I ran all the way home. I told my mother and she squinted up at the sun and said that some people had the devil in their heart without knowing it.

My husband kissed me where I stood on the porch this morning. I said I was trembling from the cold mist that crawled up from the ground and he laughed. He held me tight and promised me something sweet. His skin smelled different to Caleb's. His neck wrinkled above his shirt and I could see my thread stitching there – pale blue to go with the pale blue line through his shirt.

'Caleb', I said so soft. 'Caleb'. I said again.

His body didn't move. I checked his eyes. They stared out dead. The whole world was silent as I stood up and I saw what else I had to do.

I slowly rolled Caleb over to the river's edge and I pushed him in.

He floated. His face turned and his eyes stared out at me. I prayed he was still dead right up to the moment when the water pulled him away; and I kept watch, running along the bank, watching Caleb's body bump and roll. Not one rock stopped him and the last I saw of Caleb Mayer was his hands slowly disappearing into white water.

I saw a red-tailed hawk eating a grey squirrel on my way home. The sky was still light in the west and a wind crept from somewhere to breathe on me. 'Caleb' said some dark piece of my mind but I didn't listen. I saw my house with the chimney smoking. I saw the garden with green beans and onions. I saw the gooseberries hung all green-lit in the evening sunshine and I remembered the first time Caleb Mayer kissed me – all real and beautiful before there was ever a devil in his heart.

Longitude and Latitude

What I liked was the idea that I could die at any time if I didn't pay attention. The Captain seemed to understand this, too, as we sat smoking in the galley, our fingers close to our mouths, holding our cigarettes in.

The Captain said he understood human nature. He had learned it all from looking at men's eyes as they looked at the sea. He said even evil men could look innocent then ... and he pointed at my face.

'You've ideas on getting lost', he said. 'I've seen your kind before. Come out here and you think you can find your soul'.

The Captain was maybe about fifty, but maybe more and his face was caved in on one side. He never said what happened, but each morning he plucked stray hairs from the hard seams of flesh and cracked them between his teeth.

The first time I saw the Captain, I gave him the whole routine. I was tired of the rat race ... I lost money ... I threw away the mobile ... I always had this yen for the sea outside my window.

It was mostly lies, but I said and acted them good.

And I told him that I liked crabs. I liked their dark eyes that shifted on stalks. I liked their pincers that bit and crawled over each other and me. The thing about crabs was that they saw their world flat, but in 360 degrees. They could judge distance, could see birds flying above them and saw predators approaching from behind – things I didn't want to see, but things I knew were still there.

That night the Captain played his fingers on the plastic table cloth while I rationed out my attention on my surroundings ... the yellow/green goblin halo of the reading lamp in the corner; the television frozen with a DVD image of some woman on a dusty road, her leg paused in mid-kick at her car tyre; the galley fridge; the microwave and cooker; the smell of eggs and fat bacon; the coughing smoke filter, coughing all the way up its little chimney to the night outside ...

... then there was the edge of the sea; the shore, the city, the road leading to my old place and the easiest thing to do would be to walk right on in, but I pulled my head back from that ... I went back to the Captain's fingers, still drumming ... and in the back of my head was this idea that all I had to do was open my mouth and tell the truth.

The Captain turned his hands palms up.

'See these lines?' he asked me.

'Sure', I answered.

'Longitude and latitude', the Captain said and he drew one finger along his life-line, his love-line as well as all the other various marks, cuts and scars. 'And in between are the spaces where all the monsters and mermaids live ...'

'Oh', I said.

'Longitude and latitude', the Captain continued. 'They meet up because they can't do it any different ... something inbred needs to find its harbour. Murphy out there ... drink has ruined him and now he can't trust himself on dry land ... so he comes right to the edge … and he stays here'.

'Good for Murphy', I said.

'So what has you here?' the Captain said.

I had plans, you see, about how to determine the rest of my existence. I'd go to the absolute margins and see if I could disappear, but it didn't work out that way. The Captain wanted to know what I was and what I wanted. It was part of the job, he'd said. A man like you with hands like yours, what does he want to do with fishing?

Instead of answering, I gazed up at the girl on the frozen DVD. She had good legs, but her face was all curled up in frustration. It made her ugly. I wanted to peel her lips back into place, smooth out her cheeks, rub up her hair between my hands, make it look like a halo. She had yellow hair. Nice, I thought.

'I've seen the way you look out to sea', the Captain said.

'I like the waves', I explained.

'Murphy said you disturb the crabs'.

'The crabs are fine', I said.

The Captain looked back down at his hands.

'What did you do?' he asked, softly and there was this feeling inside me. Not penance exactly, but something close – something that just wanted me to be quiet and forgotten, to be a closed up hole in a wall, a nothing.

When I was a kid, Mum told me to go to confession.

'Irons out the soul', she used to say.

When I got older, Mum found Buddhism.

'Irons out nothing', she said in the end.

She died all narrowed up in a hospital bed, while my wife Carol stood behind me.

'You can't even hold your mother's hand', Carol accused.

So I had to hold Mum's hand just to prove I could. It was like gristle and as I rolled the last of her knuckles between my finger-tips, I looked at her face. It had withered on the bone, but I remembered how Dad used to kiss her there when he felt like it. He used to grab her hair too and she'd laugh when I'd get scared.

'It's just love darling', she'd tell me. 'Just love'.

'I think I killed my wife', I said. I swallowed some coffee then I whittled my confession down ...

'I killed my wife'.

It sounded good to say it. It sounded real. I was amazed I'd said it, but I had wanted to say right from the moment I had done it. I had wanted to scream it in the street, yet when I had reached the street, all I had noticed was the way the road just kept on going.

'I killed my wife', I said again. 'Yeah, I killed her'.

The Captain said nothing, but he rammed his hands together and lowered his head. A pulse beat under one of his scars. I could hear nothing but my own breath. It was a curious thing just to wait and see what would happen next.

Then I looked at my hands. There had been blood, but I had washed that off in the kitchen sink. Bright blood splashed on her soap, then seeped into its white sludge. I tried to get it out, but it went too deep so I poured boiling water from the kettle to soften it to nothing. Its smell made me gag. It smelled like her hands. I glanced down to where her legs were tucked up on the floor. She looked asleep.

I shoved the last of the soap down the sink's plug-hole.

'You sure?'

I looked up to see the Captain staring at me.

'Are you sure she's dead?' he asked.

I sucked up the last of bacon grease from my teeth. The galley light swayed a little and for seconds I wanted his question to mean something. So I said:

'No, I'm not'.

That's good', the Captain said. 'That's good to think that', he said.

His mouth went crooked. It might have been a smile.

I thought of my front door. I wondered how close I could get to it ... even touch the coloured lead glass panels. Red tulips with bluebells framed within a gold opaque background.

I thought of her lying on the kitchen floor. I thought of her eyes watching me as I walked around. I thought of the last real words I said to her.

'What's all this small talk', I had said, wanting to hurt her but wanting to keep her safe afterwards.

'What's all this small talk?'

And her smile had dripped off her face. She was standing in the kitchen, looking too much like Mum looked when Dad got funny – that kind of funny in his eyes, in his voice, and she and I didn't know what he was going to do. Bad funny or good funny ... and I used to watch the seconds go real slow in front of me while Mum and Dad just stood there.

'I loved him', Mum said once. 'And he loved me'.

She put her two hands together. 'Like that', she said.

And before I disappeared, I looked into the bathroom mirror and I knew I was still different from Dad. I still loved her, didn't I? I could go down and clean up her face; make her some tea; make up my promises one ... two ... three ...

Later I brought Murphy up a coffee.

'Hey Murphy', I said. 'Do you ever look at the sea?'

Murphy looked at me, then spat. 'It's just water, isn't it?'

'I thought everyone looked at the sea once they got on a boat', I said.

Murphy kept looking at me. 'You get used to it'.

I walked over to the edge and looked down at the sea as it rolled beneath me. I looked at the dirty foam and at the random bodies of seagulls caught in it, and they turned their heads up at me

I thought I saw a human face there with eyes I recognised. I thought she smiled at me. I thought she had forgiven me. Just that side of her face between her ear and her mouth where I could kiss her.

Dead People

Darren says his weird uncle has some pictures in his garage. Pictures of dead people, he says, and he looks at me. I'm smoking my last cigarette, feeling the smoke curve round my teeth.

'You want to see dead people?' Darren says.

I push my hair out of my face so I can look at Darren. He's wearing his birthday jacket. It's black with an ice-sheen. He wants me to give him a present too. Something good he says. Something he can think about before he goes to sleep. Darren thinks he's romantic. He thinks I'm his. He says he likes my mystery face. He tells his friends I'm the sort you wait for. I know he's lying. My best friend Freda said Darren waits for no-one. He didn't wait for her – but maybe you're different, Freda said.

Darren says he likes me because I've got ideas and I read books. One day he showed off how nice he was to me by asking me to read from the book in my bag.

'Who the fuck is Emily?' said Darren's friend. Josie. She chewed her gum and fingered the pages in the book.

'A writer', I said.

'See?' Darren said. 'Read a bit', he said to me.

So I read it. I can't remember whereabouts it was in the book I read, but it was good. I like all those words that say things. I like the way a sentence shows up like a picture in my head. Mum says I've got one of those minds you got to be careful about. I want too much weird stuff after reading books. Her sister was the same and she ended up dead somewhere. Mum's warned me that if I do anything with Darren ... you wash yourself out, you hear me?

Darren tries to touch me too much. He comes round to play cards with my step-dad, Kevin. Kevin says I couldn't do any better. Kevin says my books breed spiders in the house. Once Kevin hit me straight across my face and Mum just got quiet in the kitchen. She smoked that whole afternoon with the telly on. Kevin said I was the sort of girl you had to keep your eyes on.

Once I let Darren do something. He said it would be nice. It felt like a warm slug in my mouth and I threw up afterwards. Darren took a photo on his phone of my face. He said even with puke on my chin, I looked like one of the girls in the old paintings he's seen in his uncle's garage. Flat-faced girls with creamy skin and gold bands in their hair.

Freda says I look ugly sometimes. She says I don't know what girls are supposed to do for boys. You don't just kiss or lick it. You do other things as well. Things like Mum does in bed with Kevin. Mum says I'll learn someday.

So when Darren says his uncle's got pictures of dead people, I say what kind.

Darren sits up close to me. He smells dirty, but I don't tell him.

'You know', he says. 'Shit you've seen on the telly'.

He pushes holes through my cigarette smoke, then he tries to kiss me. I pull back. His teeth are yellow and there's a cold sore between his nose and his mouth. He sucks his tongue back in.

'I told him about you', Darren says. 'I said you liked books and stuff. He said to bring you over sometime'.

So I went over.

Darren's uncle looked like Darren would look like if he was in a book written by someone great. He lived in the garage because his wife hung herself after her baby died. Darren said I wasn't to mention anything about that. He said his uncle goes a bit crazy now and again and Darren's mum has to hide the knives and the bleach.

Darren's uncle smiles at me when he sees me. He puts his hand out for me to shake. I like his hand. It's very clean. He says, would you like a drink?

Darren goes over to a small fridge near a sink.

'Non-Alco', Darren's uncle says.

Darren shrugs. 'Sure, Eddie'.

His uncle gets me orange juice. I'm trying to remember Darren's surname, while his uncle shoves some magazines off a chair.

'Thanks, Mr Sheridan', I say and sit down.

He bows a little. 'Eddie', he says.

Darren says, 'I told her you had pictures of dead people'.

Darren's uncle looks funny at me.

'You don't have to show me', I say.

Darren moves back and forward. 'No, he'll show them ... won't you show them, Eddie?'

Darren's uncle shrugs. 'Okay'.

He goes over to a large bookshelf full of books. My eye goes fuzzy if I stare too much, but I want to see the names of the books. I want to open them up.

'I read books', I say out loud.

Darren's uncle looks round at me.

'She reads to me', Darren says.

I want him to shut up. I want him to disappear.

'That's good. That's nice', Darren's uncle says.

He brings a large book over to his desk near the window. Darren gets there first, but his uncle makes a space for me between him and Darren. His uncle smells clean and just before I look at the picture he's showing me, I look at the side of his face. There's no hair on his cheeks at all and, this close to him with the light from the window, I can see that he has more red in his hair than brown and his eyelashes are long and nearly red. Orange, but a nice orange. I smile a bit and he catches me.

I really hope I look just like Darren says I do, like a girl from a painting in one of his uncle's books.

'I want a cigarette', Darren says.

'Go on outside then', his uncle tells him.

Darren goes outside and lights a cigarette in front of the window.

I look down at the picture his uncle is showing me. It's black and white and it has houses in straight lines. Nothing but houses, but weird houses. Long and narrow and with barbed wire wrapped around towers. I know what this is.

'Want to see the next one?'

'Sure', I say.

I've seen pictures like these before in my history books. Darren's uncle goes through them all. He's counting the photograph pages under his breath. People who don't look like people anymore, dead, piles of skeletons with bits of skin dripping off, women who still have ankle socks on their legs, even though they are dead and men's briefcases all buckled up.

Darren comes back in. 'What do you think?' he says.

I don't say anything. I drink my orange and walk about the room. Darren's uncle follows me. He touches some flowers in a vase, then picks up a book. Darren leans against the wall and looks bored.

'You should get a telly in here, Eddie'.

'Don't want one'.

I'm standing in front of the books and Darren's uncle stands right beside me.

'You can read anything you like here', Darren's uncle says. He looks at me. 'You can come back any time'.

Afterwards Darren gets angry with me. He says maybe I want to fuck his uncle. I stop dead when Darren uses that word. It makes me go cold, right to my guts. Darren pushes me up against the wall and I want to scream, but his hand is right over my mouth. Freda says she usually just ends up thinking about something else. Something like the dress she wants in Penny's. I think hard about nothing because the pain makes me want to break. Then I think about killing Darren. I think about finding a rock and smashing his face in two and when it's over I try so hard to walk like nothing's wrong with me and Darren walks on ahead, smoking his cigarette and when I get home, I get into the hottest shower I can and I stay there until I can't feel anything anymore.

Finding Women

We kill like dogs on heat. We scrabble over smashed-down houses, sniff inside garden sheds and we enter through windows, some with their curtains nailed to the frames.

This time the curtain rags are blue with yellow spots. Foster doesn't see me touch. He's searching for food. He's also growling. He calls it singing. He opens his mouth and lets rip. It's his way of informing whoever is in hiding that he'll find them and he'll drag them out and hack them down. Yet, even as they plead for their lives, he has to reason with them. He has to re-discover his old teaching methods and re-design his face into what it used to be. 'This is war', he'd explain. 'You are on the wrong side and I have the weapon. You just have to die'.

Foster finds a bra. He fixes it across his chest. Its back straps flap as he dances around the kitchen. He finds other things as well, green mould dishcloths, a baby's cup, rotten milk in the fridge, old newspapers …

'Do you think there is anything else?' he says out loud.

'Where's Boyle?' I say.

Foster jerks his head towards the hallway, then drops back into silent mode. His face changes into straight lines. His smile dies down into nothing.

'No one here', I say.

He holds one finger up, as if he has heard something.

But it's just Boyle whistling in the background somewhere.

'No one left', I tell Foster.

Foster smiles and whispers, 'You never know'.

I follow to see him tip-toe up the stairs. I could go up and watch him find somebody, watch him kill them in his special way, but I decide to join Boyle instead.

Boyle is in the sitting room, parading the circumference of the floor and kicking odd bits of furniture out of his way. He stops whistling when he sees me.

'Nothing but crap left', he announces.

I move in. Things snap under my feet. Things like glass. They sound like bones. I stop to look down, but it's just glass. I look up again and Boyle thinks I'm looking up at the ceiling, listening to Foster as he prowl and hunts.

'Old bastard will find somebody', Boyle says. He winks at me. Boyle used to be a farmer. He said he just went out and voted differently one day and, what do you know, we got a different world all of a sudden.

Foster likes to tell us that history just joins up time until we die. Boyle says Foster is just getting old and mad.

I'm looking at the bookshelves. Sometimes I can find things in bookshelves. Bits of necklaces or dried flowers, old notes and bookmarks or photographs, and if I'm really lucky, the photographs are dated. I can work back the years from there. Ten is too far back because then I see things that don't live anymore. I see my mother's blue dress and her arm in the sun. I see my father's smile and his car in the driveway. I can even hear their voices, but it is like having goldfish open their mouths in my head.

Upstairs there is a bump, then a scream.

'He's found someone', Boyle says. He sits down on a pile of wood and books.

'Wonder what it is?' he purrs.

I shrug. It's best to shrug. It's best just to wait, then take each second as it arrives.

Boyle comes down the stairs and spins a woman into the room.

Boyle whistles. 'Nice bra', he says.

The woman falls to the floor. She's wearing a skirt and an old jumper, no shoes and her feet are freshly broken.

Foster looks at me. 'What do you think … eh?'

I don't say what I think. I don't like finding women. I shrug instead and add on a smile.

Foster kicks the woman's thigh and she raises her head only a little, but I know if she was younger, stronger and had a more quick and desperate mind, then she'd work out some way to survive beyond the next five minutes or half-an hour. The same way I also know that if some miracle happened – if we became kind, or if we liked her skin and her eyes, then maybe she'd survive for longer, but Foster says you've got to kill things that don't fit in anymore, no matter how much you want to keep them.

The woman is crying blood. She pulls her legs up. She leans forward a little to gather her destroyed feet. The pain makes her face shine beneath the blood.

Boyle stares over at her, then scratches his crotch. 'Is that all?' he says.

But Foster's glare shuts him down.

When Foster first found me he taught me that in this new life you've got to forget who you were supposed to be. Foster was supposed to be a history teacher, Boyle was supposed to remain a farmer and I was supposed to study something in a university.

'You do it this time', Foster says. He takes off the bra and stands back to watch.

The woman on the floor doesn't look like anyone I used to know, but she has small wrists and I like small wrists. My stomach goes calm and light. Foster is breathing hard. He's getting old too fast. Boyle says we should just kill the old fucker and strike out for ourselves.

Boyle lights a cigarette. He glances over at me, cool and steady. I stare at the woman on the floor. She isn't young, but she still has a good face. She curls forward onto the ground, like all she wants us to do is to cut her down to nothing.

'Attention there ...' Boyle mimics Foster's voice. 'Attention in the back of the class ... history is recyclable ... it just happens inside out and outside in ... Hitler begot Mussolini begot Mao begot Ceausescu begot Idi Amin begot Mugabe begot some other little fucker down the road ...'

'Shut up Boyle', I say.

The woman moans into the ground, as I crouch down beside her.

'Now just do it easy', Foster warns. He sits back on his heels and wipes up his sweat.

'Hey ...' I whisper. I touch her hair. I can feel how cold her skull is underneath it. 'Hey ...'

The woman turns to me. I count five seconds, before I smile. I make sure it's my best smile. The sort of smile I had for my birthdays when I was a kid.

'I bet you had a good life', I say to her. 'I bet you loved somebody'.

The woman moves her lips as if she's trying to copy my smile, centimetre by centimetre, and I know she's praying that somehow she'll get out of this alive.

'I bet you thought none of this would ever happen to you', I say.

'But history', Foster eggs on. 'History ...!'

The woman is crying now. The sound is mainly in her throat and I can feel my insides, my stomach, my lungs, even the hinges of my muscles – I can feel them all move in time to her tiny voice.

I don't like finding women.

One Thousand Selves

I have tried to lose the stray dog in the mountains, but it has followed me here to the Select Hôtel in Paris ... to these queer, cheap rooms that overlook the roofs of the Sorbonne.

I can see the sky and there are vacant windows like those vacant holes in my lungs, gobbling up my air the way a dog gobbles meat ...

... and LM is stretching to light the lamp now. She wants to tempt me with pallid egg on toast. I want champagne.

The fire licks my slippers.

I am so full of blood.

'No egg then?' LM says.

I shake my head, reach my hand to my face and she reacts.

'Are you too hot?'

She planks her body in front of me. I can see her chest. Her breasts would smother me if I let them. I stare at the small lace frill on her blouse. She smells of egg. I hold my breath and her face pushes down to look at me. Then she smiles and plumps the edges of the pillow behind my head.

'There ...' she tells me.

She pokes the fire hard and its heat climbs up my face. Sometimes I think that LM would like to preserve me here. Not really dead, but not able to live away from her either.

'Did you write any letters today, Katie?'

'I wrote to Jack', I answer.

LM tightens up her lips. I lean back against my chair and push my hands through my wrap. I would like Jack's head to be in my lap; just to hold him and make him listen.

But I've torn out the page from my journal. Even as I was writing the words I could see all of me change. All those other KM's, Katies, Japanese Kate, Russian Kate, Tinkahori Kass, falling into one thousand selves.

The self with Lawrence.

'You are a loathsome reptile', he wrote to me in Capri. 'I hope you will die'.

Jack never really saw Lawrence. I saw Lawrence.

Lawrence playing with a string between his fingers. I loved his eyebrows. How straight they were across his eyes. I used to try to straighten mine in the mirror. I tried to put myself inside Lawrence once. Closed my eyes under the sun one day and I felt the heat crawl in through my fingernails. I tried to feel all that heat boil in my heart, then roll down to between my legs. Is that what it was for Lawrence when he saw Jack? That boiling heat, ready to make flesh wrestle.

He put me as Gudren. I put him as myself.

All my selves spattering at my feet. If I look hard enough they soon disappear into the carpet; my mouths trailing into rose thorns, my eyes rolling behind rose leaves; all my faces spreading out, then being eaten by LM's shoes as she walks about the room, undoing the frill at her throat.

She stands facing the locked hotel room door and twists her fingers. She whispers something before she turns and faces me.

'Cocoa then?'

'Champagne', I tell her.

LM shakes her head, then wriggles her fingers in front of her bosom.

'No', she says. 'No ... no ... too many bubbles ... they aren't good for your lungs'.

I look towards the window. LM has not yet drawn the curtains. I'm afraid that the dog is out there waiting for me; his large paws placed one above the other; his tail a fat brush of hair and dirt. He has ticks and loose gums.

He reminds me of Wyndham, all long with the hang-dog jaws of his self-portraits. I had all my 'I's' with me when I went to to lunch with Sydney and Violet Schiff in Cambridge Square, and there was Wyndham, wiping his hands clean from painting Violet, and my 'I's' bristled beneath my skin. I felt them pull and squeeze my words as I talked. Wyndham licked his moustache. Violet smiled and Sydney poured a little wine.

'I have not read your work, Miss KM', Wyndham said. 'I have read the notices'.

I tried to like him. I tried to please him like you would a dog, but I was never fond of dogs. I prefer cats. I metioned my selves, my 'I's', running around my body like screws working a machine. I mentioned Ouspensky who had said that Leonardo and Michelangelo were not artists; but very fine machines.

'All the art we know is mechanical and subjective'.

Wyndham laughed at me. He called me a vulgar writer. My characters had sliding smiles like small sharks and lived dull café lives or hid in the New Zealand bush, brushing their hair in front of mirrors, contemplating some minor fantastical lover.

'A magazine story writer of the machine variety', he announced to Violet and Sydney, who did nothing; who only remarked on the weather for this time of year; who said how they liked Sundays and how the day was always perfectly suited to its name.

And LM was saying now:

'You have to have a little something for your birthday, Katie'.

I stare back at her. All that love for me inside her. It twists me.

I remember Granny Dyer in the bath and I wish I was a little girl again, watching Granny lift the sponge to her arms and her beautiful face. I wish I saw Maata again, or even had that moment on the ship when Papa looked at me as if he was afraid of how I was made.

And Virginia, marvelling at the words in me, using her bird's eye to mark down each word I used to describe Lady Ottoline's garden. The b*right dazzle* of tulips, the *pairs* of walkers; the conversations like music *set to flowers* ... and later in Virginia's story, it was all there, all that living light and bright air.

Who was I to her then?

'It's not too far gone, Katie'. LM was saying. 'Your birthday ...'

Her face eats me like a cow eats grass.

'Your birthday', she says again.

The words sound so lovely from her mouth. They could be real if I could just live and work and write. In Fountainebleu I will be reborn. I will be that self of all selves. None of them ever saw that self. Not LM, not even Jack, neither poor old Carco or Goodyear, nor Kot, who once gave me a bright Russian dress. Not even my brother Leslie, my Chummie ...

He and I had been walking up and down the garden in Acacia road when a pear fell from the tree. Chummie picked it up and polished it with his handkerchief. He asked if I remembered the pear tree at home and the old Southerly Buster wind that would tear them down for the ants to eat.

'We shall go back when it's all over', he promised. 'And find everything'.

I scribbled something down for him before he left. It wasn't a letter but just my arms around him. He died out there, blown to bits, showing his men how to throw a hand grenade.

In Bandol I sat and watched the red sun sink into the sea until a man found me.

'You are alone, Madame?'

'Alone, Monsieur'.

'You are living at the hotel, Madame?'

'At the hotel, Monsieur'.

'Ah, I have noticed you walking alone several times, Madame'.

'It is possible, Monsieur'.

He blushed and put his hand to his cap.

'I am very indiscreet, Madame'.

'Very indiscreet, Monsieur'.

But one self of mine – a high, wild self who wanted tear the dark red sun apart with her fingers – she wanted to say something so different.

She wanted to say. 'I am discreet. I am very discreet'.

And she wanted that quiet discreet to be nothing more than a white sheet brought over her head so she could sleep.

But she wrote for Leslie instead. She wrote about their childhood. She wrote about Kezia touching Pat the handy man's earrings – after he had chopped the head from a white duck – *'Do they come on and off?'*, and Mouse, little Mouse – *'Je ne parle pas français'* – there was a dog there too; and Beryl, the real Beryl behind the false one, a shadow behind the mirror ... *'And then after six years, she saw him again'* ...

... and Laura visiting the dead young man laid out on a table ... that strange, sly beauty Death ... then her brother Laurie ...

'Isn't life –'

But what life was she couldn't explain. No matter. He quite understoond.

'Isn't it, darling?' said Laurie.

But LM is at the curtains. She pokes her head between them, sighs, then pulls them shut.

'Is there a dog out there, Ida?' I ask her.

LM shakes her head, smiles and turns about the room, then taps her foot on the edge of the fire-place before she says:

'There is nothing out there, Katie'.

On the 16th of October, two days after her thirty-fourth birthday, Katherine Mansfield went to Fountainebleu in the hope of regaining her 'self' amongst an extended family under the guidance of George Ivanovich Gurdjieff, founder of the Institute for the Harmonious Development of Man.

'Live in your body again', Gurdjieff advised her.

She scraped carrots, inhaled cows' breath and she pinned back her fringe. On Boxing Day she wrote:

'You see, my love, the question is always: "Who am I?" ... "Is there a Me?"'

On Katherine's invitation, Jack arrived on Tuesday the 9th of January 1923, and Katherine decided to comb her fringe back down to welcome him.

After supper, she ran up the stairs ahead of him, but her lungs loosened and her blood spurted out. Jack led her to her bed and rushed for the doctor. He was pushed out of the room and Katherine died minutes after.

Sources

On pp 123–4 there is an imaginative re-working of letters and notes passed between Katherine Mansfield, Wyndham Lewis and Violet Schiff.

Letter from Wyndham Lewis to Violet Schiff at Roquebrune, 6 February 1921.

Letter from Wyndham Lewis to Violet Schiff, 20 September 1922.

Letter from Wyndham Lewis to Sydney Schiff, 20 September 1922.

Words in italics on p. 124 are from Katherine Mansfield's letter to Lady Ottoline, Wednesday 15 August 1917.

Dialogue in italics on p. 125 is from *Journal of Katherine Mansfield*, Sunday (December) 1915 – 'An Encounter'.

Prose and dialogue in italics on p. 126 is from Katherine Mansfield's 'The Prelude', 'Je ne parle pas français', 'The Dill Pickle' and 'The Garden Party'.

The Kiss

It started off just watching Timmo play with some other kids in the park. Parents were used to him by now. Although they were still wary that he was almost fourteen. Timmo liked playing with little kids. Mum had gone round to all the neighbours and showed them all the consultant reports that said he was safe to play with. She said he was the original big kid. He was a beautiful boy and he was always going to be just a boy.

'You should get him a licence', Dad said as half-a-joke. 'Make sure they know he's harmless'.

'He's got Dennis', Mum said.

I'm Dennis. I'm three years older. I've got this laugh that no one wants to like. Girls don't touch me unless I do something that makes them scared but interested all at the same time and that doesn't happen much.

But Timmo hasn't got to do anything. He just smiles and girls smile back. They like touching him because he's got soft skin and Mum makes sure he smells good. Dad says she puts too much washing powder in Timmo's clothes wash, but Mum wants him really clean. She says nothing extra about Timmo is going to make him look weird.

Timmo doesn't look weird. He looks beautiful.

'Hey, Drongo', some girl came up to me in the park and said, 'How much for a kiss from Timmo?'

I stared at her. Some little bitch with her hand on her hip, hiking her uniform nearly up over her *scungies*.

I had too much cider in my mouth, so I couldn't answer straight off.

'Been thinking about that', I said after a bit.

'Shut up, Drongo, you're just a liar', an older girl said.

That was Ruth Keating. She took my cider bottle and drank it way down, then she burped and everyone laughed. Ruth Keating is the sort of girl I don't like looking at too much because it makes me feel weird. Ruth Keating has brown hair. Bits of it go yellow in the sun. She says she puts lemon juice into it. Once she dyed her hair white blonde and it made her nose stick out.

'Get lost, Bush-Pig', I said.

I don't know if she's a Bush-Pig. I never tried to find out, but she's got boyfriends. They all say she does it quick with really cute noises.

Ruth Keating smiled and put her face up close to me and I could smell how warm her neck was. I turned and bit her. She squealed and jumped back, but I could see she wasn't all that scared.

'Jesus, Drongo', the first girl said. 'No one wants to kiss you'.

'Alright ... how much then?' Ruth said.

I looked across to where Timmo was playing with a dead butterfly.

'Five dollars', I told them.

That's how it started.

The thing is Timmo likes being touched. Mum said it was a side effect from his brain not being as developed as it was supposed to be. Dad said maybe it was that time she disappeared to the Gold Coast, never rang, never did a damn thing until Dad hunted her down in some B&B, found her out the back door in some shit-hole garden and pregnant, with some man painting her toe-nails for her.

Some nights Dad goes cold and quiet and rubs Timmo's head like he wants to rub it out.

The neighbourhood girls don't rub Timmo that way but they pay five dollars a go to kiss and touch him. I put the money in a small box and hide it in our wardrobe. Timmo wants an aeroplane. I want a car.

Timmo's got these shoulders that girls like to hang onto and they like to run their fingers up and down his ribs. Mum keeps Timmo on a strict diet. His type get fat, she said. 'You take him for walks, Dennis'. I make Timmo walk for miles. We walk as far as West Ryde, then circle back down through Eastwood and back up home. Sometimes we take the train into the City. We get off at Town Hall and walk up and down. Most times, women give me nice looks. I take extra special care of Timmo because women like to see me being gentle. I even get my voice down low and soft.

Some women pay for our dinner. Nothing much ... chips mostly, but now and again you meet a woman who just wants something extra from us. I know how to suss them out. They hang about the National Gallery or the Botanical Gardens and even in some of the art galleries in Kings Cross. We don't do Darling Harbour much. It's too full of cops looking interested. But we take the ferries sometimes and hang about the railings. Timmo makes faces at the seagulls. I check out the women. I like ones with black hair and scarves tied round their necks. Blondes are okay, but women with dark hair – they look at you different.

Some women come up close and say 'What are you boys looking at?'

I tell them we're on a holiday, or waiting for our Dad to finish up with business somewhere. Timmo has learnt the routine off by heart. His face goes soft. He doesn't cry, but he makes his lips wobble. Sometimes he shakes. It's good but. It adds to the atmosphere.

Most women go for Timmo, but some go for me.

One of them said I must love Timmo so much since I look after him so well. I shrugged and said 'Sure'. She smiled and handed me a glass of watered-down wine.

She said, 'French children drink that all the time'.

'You French?' I said.

'Not really', she said.

She didn't sound French. She just sounded English with a bit of Australian on the edges. Her name was Elizabeth and she had black hair.

I kept on drinking the wine. I like wine. It's different to cider. Cider fizzes up against your teeth, wine just slicks down, down to places I like.

Elizabeth said. 'I saw a woman in Lyons give her son wine like that once'. She tapped my fingers with her knife.

'You like it, don't you?'

I rolled 'Lyons' in my head. I hadn't really heard it before. I heard of Darwin, then further on into Osaka, then a bit further.

Mum says she likes going places when she gets down. She makes sure we've got food in the freezer. She's good like that. We can always tell when she's getting ready to ditch us. She puts on more make-up and she gets all happy. She dances with Timmo, dances with me.

I ask, 'When you coming back, Mum?'

She laughs and says, 'Where did I go wrong with the both of you?'

Me all practical, Timmo all dumb.

Mum got on a plane to Russia once with some guy she met in a pub near the Rocks. She sent a postcard from St Petersburg. She said it had an angel. She brought us back key-rings. Dad said, 'Who'd you go with?' He said he loved her first. Mum turned round to him in the kitchen, undid her top, took Dad's fist and pushed it hard in between her bra.

'See this here?' she said. 'You just don't fill it anymore'.

Mum and Dad did things like that in front of Timmo and me and, if it got bad, I took a stubbie from the fridge and Timmo would go all baby on me and crawl into my bed.

Sometimes I'd push him right up against the wall just so I wouldn't have to touch him and I wouldn't have to listen to him breathe and fart in his sleep. I shut down so nothing of him got into me.

Elizabeth liked Timmo. She sprinkled his chips with salt and said, 'You got everything you need, Timothy?'

'You could kiss me', I told Elizabeth. She smiled and played with her sun-glasses.

'Maybe you're too young', she said. She looked around the restaurant. 'At best they think you're my younger brother'. She looked at Timmo. 'Brothers', she added.

'We do this all the time', I said.

I don't always go straight in there with the truth, but sometimes my head has different ideas to what I usually say. Elizabeth took us up to her room and she ran a bath for Timmo.

'Is he safe in the water?' she asked.

'He's alright', I said. 'As long as you leave the door open'.

Elizabeth took off her earrings, then her dress. Some women move like snakes when they use their hips. I sat on the bed and she sat down beside me. I could smell roses off her.

Elizabeth touched my face. 'How did you get a name like Drongo?'

I moved my face so she could touch it more.

'I laugh funny', I said. 'Kids in school said I sound like a dingo on drugs. You put the two words together and there's "Drongo", right?'

After we had done it she got dressed and brushed her hair.

'You got a girlfriend?'

'No', I said.

'You should', she said. 'You've got good fingers'.

She dried Timmo off, then dressed him. He kissed her like he kisses Mum, and Elizabeth looked at me and said, 'Is there a charity I can give money to, for Timmo?

'Just me', I said and held out my hand.

She gave me fifty dollars and buttoned up my shirt, then she tucked it in.

We got off the train at Eastwood. Timmo was tired. He said his skin itched.

'She must've used a different shampoo on you', I said.

'Hey, Timmo', someone called.

It was Ruth Keating. She left some guy by his car and crossed over to us.

'Hey Drongo', she said. 'See that guy behind me?'

I looked ... blonde and big, bare feet under surfer shorts and a necklace. He was talking into his phone.

'Okay', I said.

She said, 'Five dollars, right?'

'You making *him* jealous?' I said.

'Just a bit', she said.

'He's not looking', I told her.

'He'll look', Ruth said.

She stood on her tip-toes to reach Timmo's face. She was wearing gold thongs and her toe-nails were polished purple.

'Five dollars', I reminded her.

'In my pocket', she said.

She jutted one of her elbows towards her left-hand pocket. I shoved my hand in and pressed my knuckles on her hip before I flicked the five dollars from her pocket.

'Timmo knows how to kiss me', Ruth said. 'Don't you, Timmo?'

Swear to God, I never saw it coming. Mum said I was useless. I was supposed to be Timmo's lookout. He's doesn't have a real brain, she yelled at me afterwards. He can't be held responsible.

Timmo was scratching his face just when Ruth started kissing him.

And then there was a crack, then there was blood and Ruth was screaming. Timmo's head down on Ruth's face. He had just wanted to stop the itching and her mouth had got in the way.

Ruth doubled up on the ground. She was screaming so hard that Timmo started screaming too.

'She's dead, Drongo', he screamed. 'She's dead'.

I knelt down next to Ruth. 'She's not dead, Timmo ... she's just playing'.

I could see Ruth's eyes move behind her fingers. I put the tip of one of my fingers in between hers and wiped away some blood.

Mum says I can be gentle sometimes. Mum says I shouldn't forget to be gentle.

Mum went mental afterwards. She called the doctor, then said maybe we can get another consultant. She wanted a lawyer too. Dad said, 'What for? Half the kid's brain is gone'. Mum screamed at him, 'He's your son. He's your bloody son'.

Dad said, 'Are you sure, Helen?'

Mum put her wine glass down. She said, 'What ever do you mean, Andrew?'

Mum isn't too much of an alkie, but when she's scared or angry and, when she gets slurry, she gets extra polite. Dad calls it her de-balling technique and he smiles when he says that – like he doesn't really mind it or he's just got so used to it because he says he loves her.

'You know what I mean, Helen'.

I was counting my money when Dad came to me and Timmo's bedroom door.

'What are you doing, Dennis?'

I was quick but. I stuffed some up my sweater sleeve, counted to five fast, then turned round to Dad with the box open in my hands. He could see there was about eighty dollars there in fivers and tens and small change, 'cause Timmo likes his lollies.

'Saving for Timmo', I said.

Dad looked at me. 'What for?' he said.

I thought of Elizabeth, then I thought of Mum. I jerked my head at Timmo sitting on his bed.

'His brain', I said. 'For his charity'.

Dad laughed. 'Charity!' He picked up the money and folded it into his pocket.

'Pay a few bills', he said.

'Okay, Dad'.

'Don't tell your Mum'.

'No, Dad', I said.

Then Dad looked at Timmo. 'You'll be alright. Won't you, Timmo?'

Timmo nodded.

Dad turned to go, then he said, 'Mum wants you to bring Timmo over to apologise'. He looked at Timmo's face. 'You keep him off the lollies from now on, Dennis. All that sugar sends him crazy'.

So we got to the Keating's house door and I knocked on the fly screen.

I could see all the way down the hall. The kitchen was at the end and the door was half open. A woman's voice came out from behind it.

She called out, 'Someone's at the door, Russ!'

A man came up the hall. Ruth's dad. When he recognised us, he leaned against the open door and kept on chewing his dinner. He said 'What do you two want?'

I put my hands on Timmo's shoulders. 'He's come to apologise', I said. 'Me too', I said. 'I should have watched out more. Sorry'.

Ruth's father stared at Timmo. 'Maybe he shouldn't be let out'.

'It was an accident, Mr ... Keating'. I said. I kept my voice really gentle. I even made out I could nearly cry.

Mr Keating stared at me. 'You're the one they call Drongo, right?'

'That's right'.

Mr Keating rubbed his forehead against the edge of the fly screen door. 'Her nose went clean off its axis', he said. He glanced over at Timmo who was playing with one of his toy cars that he'd brought along.

Timmo smiled at Mr Keating.

Mr Keating said, 'Nice little bugger when he smiles'.

'Timmo likes people', I said.

'Alright', Mr Keating said. He yelled 'Ruth!' then looked at me. 'Don't laugh at her', he warned. 'She's sensitive about the bandages. She's going to look different, you know'.

'I won't'.

When Ruth came to the door all I saw were the bandages.

Mr Keating said, 'You kids stay on the veranda'.

He kissed Ruth on her head, then he went back into the house. He left the kitchen door open.

'Timmo's sorry', I said loud enough so her Dad could hear me.

I moved closer to Ruth and she moved back just a little.

'Timmo's sorry', I said again. 'Aren't you, Timmo?'

Timmo looked up from his car.

'Sorry', I told him.

'Sorry', he copied me.

Ruth said nothing, but she sat down on the veranda step.

I sat down next to her. I looked at her face, then looked away.

'I'm sorry too', I said.

Timmo's played with his car. 'Vroom ... vroom ... vroooooom'.

Ruth had her fingers in her lap. Her hair smelled of food.

'You'll look really beautiful when the bandages come off', I promised her.

Ruth turned. She looked at me. Her skin had gone black and green under her eyes and I just kissed her. I smelled the medicine from the bandages, so I held my breath and I just kissed her.

About the Author

Órfhlaith Foyle was born in Nigeria to Irish parents and now lives in Galway. Her first novel, *Belios,* was published in 2005 by The Lilliput Press to critical acclaim. The same year Arlen House published *Revenge,* a collection of her short fiction and poetry.

Her first full poetry collection, *Red Riding Hood's Dilemma,* was published by Arlen House in 2010 and was short-listed for the Rupert and Eithne Strong Award in 2011.

Somewhere in Minnesota is her debut short fiction collection. She is currently working on her second novel.

For more information please see:
orfhlaithfoyle.blogspot.com